Night of the Mannequins

ALSO BY STEPHEN GRAHAM JONES

COLLECTIONS

Bleed into Me: A Book of Stories
The Ones That Got Away
Zombie Sharks with Metal Teeth
Three Miles Past
States of Grace
After the People Lights Have Gone Off
The Faster Redder Road

NIGHT OF THE MANNEQUINS

STEPHEN GRAHAM JONES

A TOM DOHERTY ASSOCIATES BOOK

NEW YORK

NIGHT OF THE MANNEQUINS

Copyright © 2020 by Stephen Graham Jones

Cover design by Catherine Casalino

Edited by Ellen Datlow

A Tor.com Book
Published by Tom Doherty Associates
120 Broadway
New York, NY 10271

www.tor.com

Tor® is a registered trademark of
Macmillan Publishing Group, LLC.

ISBN 978-1-250-75206-2 (ebook)
ISBN 978-1-250-75207-9 (trade paperback)

First Edition: September 2020

for my brother Spot, who's there

Night of the Mannequins

1

SO SHANNA GOT A new job at the movie theater, we thought we'd play a fun prank on her, and now most of us are dead, and I'm really starting to feel kind of guilty about it all.

I'd like to say it wasn't my idea, that we all thought of it spontaneously, just started saying parts of the prank out loud that jigsawed together in the air, one quarter my plan, a quarter Danielle's, Tim and JR competing to finish out the rest.

It was kind of only me, though.

Let me explain.

First, Shanna's job at the movie theater, the big one down by the lake. Her mom was making her do it. Not work—Shanna's had jobs since she was in junior high—but working there specifically, her checks going straight home to pay for what happened to their side lawn, which is a whole different thing and not my fault at all, not completely. The reason it was that movie theater and not the dollar show or the drive-in or the even bigger cineplex farther down 30 toward Dallas was, first, it was that that one's the main one in Rockwall, and closest, but, second, and probably the real reason, Shanna's mom had dated that theater's main security guard in high school, and he could keep an eye on his long-ago ex-girlfriend's daughter. He *thought*.

Two weekends in, Shanna used her usher powers to sneak us in the emergency exit at the back of theater 14, the last one on that side, and the farthest from the manager's offices, which is where security was. It was less because we wanted to see a movie than that we wanted the thrill of not paying for a movie. You know. Anyway, with assigned seating, we were having to move the four of us to a new place with about every third clump of people who came in. It was kind of a giveaway, ended up with the assistant manager coming in to count heads, and us claiming we'd thrown our ticket stubs away already, who keeps ticket stubs? The only problem was we couldn't remember where our seats had been.

It probably would have worked, or, it *could* have worked, but then the assistant manager asked us what movie this even was, surely we knew that, right?

Not really.

Worse, it turned out to be a senior citizen kind of movie—four old dudes escaping their nursing homes and doting children and county jail situations to have one last golf game—which was when we all kind of shrugged and gave up. Better to get busted than claim having wanted to see that.

Because we were sophomores the same as Shanna, it didn't take long before they were asking her questions about did she maybe know us. Of course we all temp-unfriended her while being perp-walked out, but that didn't erase snapshots, and there were a lot of those. Even under the filters and markups, it was kind of obviously the five of us, from elementary on up until this very night, including one group selfie from our stolen seats, posted right on her timeline.

So, the result of us sneaking in and not *knowing* to sit in the very front row until the show started was (A) Shanna would now work in tandem with a more trusted "experience provider," and (B) there would be random head counts of all movies she was in charge of.

It was bullshit, especially since she could be making more in tips at the car wash with Danielle—because of the Porta-Potty situation, girls didn't work there so much, so they pulled tens and even twenties sometimes—but she still had six hundred to go in paying her mom's landscaping tab, so she was stuck.

Anyway, the prank.

JR lives kind of out in the sticks, right? Way out on Rabbit Ridge, technically in Heath? Back behind his fence, there's this big hill we used to always roll down in boxes. Stupid kid stuff, pretty much turned us into in-stant chigger-bait, so we were looking like we had pim-ples before we even really had them. Anyway, in sixth grade Tim was going for the record in his box, and it crashed him through the trees, into the dark stinky muck of the creek that had never been actual water, had always been just mud.

None of us went in there anymore since Danielle had gotten poison oak or ivy or we didn't know, so we were all standing there waiting when Tim came back limping, bleeding from the forehead, and carrying a pale white arm kind of bent in cheery fashion at the elbow.

We braved the woods to see the rest of this.

There in the black slime of the creek bed was a naked white mannequin, this giant Ken Doll reaching for the sky with the one arm he had left.

You better believe he was our toy for that whole summer.

We traded him between our houses, carrying him a piece at a time bungee-corded to skateboards and bikes, or stuffed halfway into a camping backpack. We stole our dads' clothes to dress him up, leave him here and there. He had so many names, but he was finally just "Manny," for, you know, mannequin. Real clever, I know.

When we finally got bored with him, he ended up in my garage, straddling the Kawasaki 750 my dad had laid over, the motorcycle forbidden by my mom from ever being ridden again, but that didn't mean Dad had to sell it, which is a whole thing with them, but never mind.

So, Manny was a joke from when we'd been kids, before life had gotten all serious and SAT. Me having the idea to bring him back for this perfect prank was a way of honoring the kids we'd been, I figured. And it would be one last blast for Manny. Better, Shanna would get the joke right off. That was very important. It was kind of how we'd be telling her we were sorry for the hot water at her new job. Well, and for the landscaping she was paying off *with* that job too. For a lot of stuff, okay? I mean, she'd always been the toughest of us, the meanest when she needed to be, the least likely to cry or complain about cuts or scrapes, the best at earning WoodScouts badges, but that didn't mean she didn't like nice things too, we figured. Like being included in the prank to end all pranks, the one that could, someday, summarize our whole high school experience and, right now, blast us off into the future in the most fitting way.

So, we raided our dads' closets again, and dug into the costume trunk in our old fort that nobody'd found yet, way back in the trees behind Holy Trinity. We were needing clothes for Manny, but for us as well.

We were going nineties-baggy for that Friday night.

Danielle shoved a whole mannequin arm down the leg

of the pants she was wearing, which kind of made us all . . . look away but not look away? I mean, okay, Danielle was always just one of us, a girl, yeah, whatever, but she'd never been like a dating prospect, right? Mostly because none of us were dating, didn't need boyfriends or girlfriends since we had each other. Or maybe we just didn't have the nerve, were hiding in the safety of friendship, I don't know. It doesn't matter now. And Shanna was like my third cousin on my mom's side anyway. But, Danielle, the thing with her, why she'd never been in the realm of possibility—it was probably that we'd all seen each other with snotty noses in elementary, we'd all ridden the acne highway of junior high together, and now we were telling each other horror stories about the swarm of college questions constantly spewing up from the mouths of grandparents and family friends. It's like we were too close for anything romantic, if that makes sense? Any of us going out with any of the rest of us had never been a real consideration, or even a distant maybe.

Still, seeing that mannequin arm reach down the front of her pants? I had to kind of look far, far away, I don't know about Tim and JR. Then she did the same with the other arm, and tied bandannas around her thighs to keep the arms in place, and part of me was wondering why we hadn't been playing this particular game for a long time already.

"That's two limbs," JR said, all helpfully.

The legs were a thousand times trickier.

We ended up in Tim's uncle's shop in the old part of Rockwall, his uncle using a band saw to slice the legs in half top to bottom *and* longways, then drilling holes for dowels so they could be pushed back together. Because we'd told him about the joke we were playing on Shanna, he comped us a roll of duct tape to hold the legs back together. When we were leaving he shook his head, said it must be great to be young and endlessly stupid.

He's a good guy, really. If I were ever going to be his age, I think I'd want to be just like him, mostly.

Anyway, with the legs cut into pieces like that, Tim got both lower parts into his biggest backpack and slung one of his dad's shirts over it. It looked fake as hell, but would anybody at concessions risk asking the hunchback kid if he was smuggling something in or not?

JR used his old soccer bag for most of the other leg pieces, and we duct-taped it to his middle, for a stomach, because two hunchbacks in one screening might be pushing it. I picked up the last foot, hefted it under my arm, looked ahead to the uncertain future.

"You just going to carry it, Sawyer?" Danielle said like the challenge it most definitely was.

I nodded yeah, and it wasn't a lie. What I did was wrap it in cardboard and brown packing tape. My story was going to be it was a lamp my mom had wanted me to pick up from the repair place, and the window on my car—I don't have a car—it wouldn't roll up, and I couldn't leave it in the parking lot, could I?

My bet was that, while the theater might have new rules about carrying backpacks and stuff in, it wouldn't have a repaired lamp policy. And once anybody hefted it once or twice, it would obviously not be some crazy assault weapon. JR couldn't get away with this, since his dad was a known gun nut and all, so people just assumed he had some of those bullet-shaped genes, but my dad was mostly concerned with figuring out what kind of mileage our new electric car was getting, and how much that was saving us per month, per year, and on into the hybrid future, so I wouldn't get any second looks, could tap-dance right past the box office with whatever, I was pretty sure.

To prove it, I just dropped the head into a plastic shopping bag, so it was completely seeable to anyone who gave it half a look. But if you saw a human head in the bag of someone in line for a fountain drink, would *you* say anything? I mean, if I were the one holding that bag, and my record was super spotless, all my emotional meltdowns far in the past?

You wouldn't give me a second look. Probably not even a first look. Nobody would.

The torso we put in a trash bag we rubbed actual trash

all over, then leaned up against the wall in the alley by the emergency exit. It was theater 4; Danielle had coasted by the box office, checked that out for us, her hair all in her face so she was just any girl on another Friday night.

We got in without any hassle, *paid* this time, were even in the theater early enough to pop the emergency exit door without any problem—Tim did a big fake fall on the stairs on the opposite side up high, his drink going everywhere, JR acting offended and maybe ready to fight about it, nobody looking over to me holding the door open so Danielle could drag a suspicious trash bag in.

We waited until the trailers to assemble Manny, but had to lie down in front of the very front row to do it. It was gross. Our hair and shirts kept sticking to the floor, and we knew the story about the senior football players sitting in the back row and peeing in secret, letting it run all the way down to the screen, where we were.

When it was done, our throats raw from how much we had to cough to cover the duct tape tearing, each of us took an assigned article of extra clothing off, dressed Manny up, topping his outfit off with my dad's Redskins cap he wore all ironically for working in the garage, that I was sure he'd never miss, and would probably be better without.

On the count of three, then, when the screen seemed darkest, we stood with him, carry-walked him up to the seat we'd bought him, even going so far as to thumb his ticket stub into the front pocket of his shirt like a handkerchief square.

We didn't know if this was Shanna's theater or not—she never found her assignments out until she came in, and then it could change for no real reason—so the way we picked it was by what movie we actually wanted to see.

It was part three of a juggernaut of a superhero series, and we'd seen the first two about ten times already, tracking it from this theater to the dollar show to the drive-in to rentals and bootlegs—not necessarily in that order.

It was Manny's first experience at the theater, of course.

He never blinked.

2

WE SHOULD HAVE GUESSED what was going to happen next. What had to happen.

We were all hopeful and stupid, though. And, yeah, probably feeling kind of bulletproof. One of our friends worked here, didn't she? What could go wrong? And it wasn't like we hadn't paid this time. Sure, we were sort of banned, but did the assistant manager really expect that to hold? Would he rather we pirate everything on his marquee? Wouldn't that ruin the movie industry and contribute to juvenile delinquency, sir?

Anyway, about halfway through the movie, JR went down to concessions, filled his small fountain drink cup up with blue Icee and volunteered to the junior taking his money that someone had just sneaked into theater 4, was disturbing the peace, saying the lines out loud with the heroes and heroines, I don't know how he phrased it. It worked, that's what's important. A few minutes later the assistant manager *and* the manager rolled in with Shanna's mom's security-guard ex, their grim faces on, flashlights in hand, two or three experience providers ranged out behind them to get some more experience. But then, after some whispering, the ex ducked out, the rest of them waiting there along the curtain-wall so patiently, the assistant manager's loafer tap-tap-tapping to get this started already. About thirty seconds later the quiet little lights under the stair steps dialed up *bright*-bright, some people in the audience gasping, and then the footlights sucked back the complete other way, to blackness, and took all the little hidden lights along the walls down with them, stranding the theater in about five seconds of inky black, except for the exit sign, which I guess never goes off. It was weird, kind of made me feel like my whole seat was floating away with me, that *all* the seats had let go, and we were drifting up wherever now, were going to probably slam down when the lights came on.

Or maybe it was just me and my heart, I don't know.

My coke wasn't coming up through its own straw anyway, and popcorn wasn't drifting around at eye level. It was probably just the weirdness of being in a public place with so many people, and then suddenly being all alone too, if that makes any sense.

Except for that green flickering exit sign.

I used it for my anchor, told myself it *wasn't* getting smaller, that it *wasn't* sinking away from me, and held on to it as best I could until the security-guy ex at the light switches found the balance, brought the stair lights up a smidge, like he'd probably been told to.

And, in this new glow—*yes*. Just like we'd each been praying, one of the experience providers who'd been roped into this was Shanna. She was wearing the black slacks she'd borrowed from Danielle, that Danielle said she never wanted back, they were all cinemucked up, and she had the green transparent visor on that everybody from the theater was wearing to promote that new bank teller movie or whatever. It's not important. And while she didn't see me—I've thought and thought about this—I'm pretty sure she maybe did see Danielle, and kind of tried to look away like *uh-oh*.

As it turned out, "uh-oh" was right.

The manager and the assistant manager were ducking up and down the rows now, and we were all in our far-from-each-other/we're-not-a-group strategically distant unguilty seats just trying to enjoy the movie we *paid* for, and each ticket stub that showed up under a dim flash-light was one ticket stub closer to us fizzing over with so much held-back laughter.

We'd put Manny in the best seat in the house, of course. That translates to about the hardest one to get to. And, since the manager was working from the top, the assistant manager from the bottom, it was also just about the last. I guess maybe the idea was that, in a house half full like that one was, it being the fifth or sixth week of the movie already, the best seats would have been taken already, meaning the sneakers-in would have to take what's left.

I was already planning how I wasn't going to say directly to Shanna that this was my idea, but she'd be able to connect the dots. We all knew which of us still *had* Manny, right?

It was going to be perfect, wonderful, legendary.

Until the assistant manager actually got to that middle seat.

I couldn't see Danielle's or Tim's or JR's eyes, Shanna's either, but I could feel them looking at me, and each other.

What we expected was for the assistant manager to startle and fall over the back of the seat in front of him, hopefully into someone's popcorn, which he'd then have to replace, or we expected him to immediately start trying to administer the CPR Shanna said she'd had to get certified in, in case of Milk Dud failure or whatever.

Instead, the assistant manager lowered his flashlight down below knee level like he'd been doing to see stubs and not blind everyone in the place, and then he nodded, kept crouching along that row.

What the hell, right? What the fuckity fuck.

I stood up from my seat to, I don't know, to call foul,

to explain the joke and how wonderful it had been about to be, but as soon as I did the dude behind me grumbled for me to sit, so I sank back down. But it was like my chair was still floating away, right? This. Did. Not. Track. Not even a little. Yes, Manny *had* a ticket, that was going to be the next part of the joke, one of us peeling it up from his shirt pocket, but Manny couldn't flash his *own* ticket. All Manny could do was sit there.

And had the assistant manager not clocked that frozen-in-place face, that empty expression, that Ken Doll drugged-out happiness?

I shook my head no, no, this wasn't right, this wasn't even in the general arena of being *close* to right. If—if this prank wasn't working, then . . . then nothing held, right? Nothing was real. Everything was cut loose and falling just wherever, it didn't matter because rules didn't count anymore.

And then, in the middle of me forgetting how to breathe, how to process, how to not run shrieking away into permanent crazyland, the assistant manager got to me to check my ticket. Just because he was authority and I was banned, I kept my face down kind of on automatic, let him do his necessary thing and slide right past, but then Tim, a few seats down, he couldn't find his stub anywhere. Which pretty much figured for him. In trying to explain that he'd really paid, the assistant manager finally figured out who he was, which instantly turned into a big thing, Shanna getting reeled into it all unawares, both of them getting marched down the carpeted stairs.

I hardly looked up when they were led past, practically in cuffs. I just scooched my knees over to the side, kept my face down.

For the rest of the movie, then, in the dead space after the failed and failing prank, in the impossible afterplace of everything having gone wrong, I wasn't checked in to the whole superhero parade on-screen. What I *was* glued one hundred and fifty percent to was the man sitting up so straight in the center of the movie theater, his red-and-white cap on at the same rakish angle I'd put it on him, all my hopes and dreams packed into his twenty-five pounds of department store plastic, my heart beating so hard, my eyes so laser-focused, my mouth so dry, everything I thought I knew dripping out my ear, my nose, my fingertips.

When the credits rolled, Manny didn't wait for the tag-on scene we knew came later, he just stood up, didn't look around, and filed out with the rest of the crowd, his legs stiff but moving, his arms swinging in a limited range, like action-figure arms.

I leaned over, threw up into and through the bottom of my cupholder, and then smushed my cup down into it like to hide it.

3

ON THE LONG WALK home, up through the wide streets of the Richie Rich mansions, Danielle and JR were jittery with ideas for what could have happened. The reason Tim and Shanna weren't there was that they were in movie jail, the kind you only get bailed out of under the withering glare of the mom or dad you have to use your one call for.

Danielle was ninety percent sure Manny getting up and walking out had been a double prank, which I didn't think was really a thing. Her idea was that some college kids had seen what we were smuggling in, and they'd crept over, laid Manny down into the aisle and pulled him down to the door little by little, smuggled him out that way, a piece at a time probably, then creeped his outfit back in on someone else during a big action scene. For who knows what reason. Is it just automatic to steal any mannequin you happen to encounter?

"We would have," Danielle countered.

JR and me shrugged, couldn't exactly deny that.

JR's idea was that the assistant manager had actually

recognized either Danielle or me or JR or Tim, and somehow immediately figured out exactly what we were doing, there being nothing new under the sun, whatever that stupid song is. Anyway, when he'd shined his assistant manager light down for the ticket stub, he'd just been miming it. Or, he'd really done it, but we couldn't see if he was shining his light onto a ticket stub or just his own open palm.

Then, maybe because there's a secret door for the projector in back or something, he'd sneaked Manny out, switched clothes, and sneaked back in, sat in that same place, only ducking into the hat at the last moment. Just to teach us a lesson, via freaking us out.

"It worked," Danielle said, mostly talking about me, I think, since my muscles kept twitching and jerking with nerves, like I was about to burst—it was my third day of forgetting my meds, I guess I should say. They usually tamp my nerves down so people can't see them.

Not tonight, though. Tonight my insides were on full display.

"But what did he do with *Manny*, then?" my stupid nerves made me ask.

JR studied me for maybe five seconds, like he was trying to make sense of my question, and then he didn't have an answer.

"What do you think then, Einstein?" he said.

It was what they'd been calling me since I'd started taking AP courses, which my mom said would calm me down, keep my brain clicking on other stuff instead of obsessing about all the wrong stuff and then having to recount it for whoever would listen. So, "Einstein," yeah. You can't do anything about a name that's both an insult and a compliment. AP *had* kept my mind occupied somewhat, though. Until this.

"We don't know anything about him, do we?" I said to the two of them.

"The assistant manager?" Danielle said. "My mom says he played basketball the year we went to regionals, but he didn't start."

"*Manny,*" I told her.

"What do you mean?" JR asked, his mouth Icee-blue.

"Maybe somebody hadn't just thrown him away in the mud, yeah?" I said, looking them both in the eyes to really set it, JR first, then Danielle. "Maybe he'd been there forever, and he finally just, like, got uncovered."

"He looks exactly like the ones in the window where my aunt works," Danielle said.

"He's probably mad from not having a—you know," JR said, miming a penis like he was holding a fire hose. Danielle averted her eyes, rolled them like girls do.

"I'm serious," I said, then waited a kind of campfire-tale amount of time before adding, "I didn't put him on my dad's motorcycle. And I know my mom didn't. She says he's creepy, all pasty white like that."

"That leaves just one obvious person," Danielle said, tapping her chin in fake thought. "However shall we solve this impossible mystery?"

"My dad loves that bike," I said, all serious. "He wouldn't—he wouldn't make it a joke like that."

"So Manny was trying to ride away?" JR asked, a hint of nervousness to his voice.

"My dad almost died on that bike," I said right back, a hint of insult to *my* voice.

When you're talking about your dad being in the hospital for three weeks, nobody can say anything back for about ten seconds.

"Why does he even keep it?" JR asked.

"It's this whole big stupid thing," I told him, not wanting to go into it.

"Maybe somebody kicked him out of a plane," Danielle said. "Manny, I mean. That little airport's right there, isn't it?"

"That *dentist* airport?" I asked, after the beat it took to place it in my head, all the way on the other side of the interstate.

"Maybe they kicked a *person* out," JR said, falling in, "and, on the way down, the only spell he could cast to save himself was to become a mannequin."

"Because that's a spell all wizards memorize," I said. "And also because wizards are real. I'm trying to be serious here. Y'all weren't sitting at the same angle I was. I saw *Manny* stand, I saw *Manny* walk away."

"His legs are put together with little pieces of wood," Danielle said, I guess trying to be the adult of us or something.

"And he just has a bulge," JR said, leading with his pelvis again, most definitely *not* being our grown-up.

"He was our friend for that whole summer," I said. "And then we just forgot him."

Neither of them could argue with that.

We all three kind of shrugged, and we were bad enough people we didn't even call Tim or Shanna that night, and then Shanna kind of quit calling us altogether that week—she'd done it before, to punish us—and Tim was so grounded he didn't have access to any kind of phone.

Maybe this is how it happens after high school, right? Or even on the ramp up to high school being over. You just drift away, and then it gets easier not to call, and then you forget the number, and then you see your old friend in line for the movie or whatever and you let your eyes keep moving, because it's going to be awkward now. Never mind that they know you better than any other human in the world. Never mind that they fake-spilled juice into your lap in fourth grade when you'd peed your pants. Never mind that you hugged them when they slept over and cried about their dad moving out. Never mind a thousand things.

I don't know, I really don't.

We'll never get to that awkward stage anyway. Obviously.

*Un*obviously? Neither me nor Danielle nor JR looked behind us that walk home that night, but if we would have, I bet we would have seen a tall male form standing behind us, watching us from under the brim of his Redskins cap, his pants and shirt and shoes not even close to matching, his blue eyes painted wide open and intense. His posture absolutely perfect.

4

SHANNA WAS THE FIRST TO GO. And by "go" I mean *die*. And by "die" I mean *get killed*.

It's like—she was still part of us, I guess, of the group that had abandoned Manny one perfect summer so long ago. So, Manny, he was starting on the outside or something, starting with her because she was furthest from the actual prank, and he was going to work his way in.

Leaving guess who right in the gooey middle, surprise.

Anyway, yeah, news flash, Shanna died when that Mack truck veered off the service road, jammed through her bedroom wall, kept right on going through the rest of her house. Big disastrophe, horrible tragedy, made *The Dallas Morning News,* her mom and little brother both dead too, whole community in tears, candlelight vigils, memorials, half days at school, the whole deal. "Why *them*?" everyone was asking. "What did *they* ever do to deserve this?" "Isn't it so random how that can happen to just anyone?" "It could have been any one of us, couldn't it have?"

There were no answers, of course, but it wasn't because there weren't answers. It was because nobody was asking me what I might know.

Would I have even told them, though?

Honestly, at that point in things, I'm not sure.

Whatever I would have said, though, it's a sure thing they wouldn't have believed me. There's not one half of one tenth of a sliver of a chance that they wouldn't have called me crazy from grief, suffering from survivor's guilt, acting out via conspiracy theories, engaging in magical thinking, maybe even showing the front edge of a psychotic break with reality, a break due to, I don't know, to our failed prank, and how it had fundamentally upset the nature of what I'd been foolishly calling reality, the one, you know, where mannequins don't get up, walk around.

It's probably good I kept quiet, I'm saying.

But I could have told them all a thing or two, if they'd wanted to listen. Or, I'd have asked them certain leading questions. What if that truck wasn't random? What if Shanna's mom and brother were just collateral damage? Most important, especially as it still applied to me and Danielle and Tim and JR, what if Shanna sort of maybe *had* been asking for it?

As far as I knew—as far as they said, and we believed them, why would Shanna and Danielle lie—Manny had been their first kiss, one truth-or-dare afternoon. And that whole summer was a . . . I don't know what the best joke had been. There were just so many, each more fabulous and inventive than the last. Setting Manny up in old people's yards holding their spraying garden hose with one hand, the other lifted to wave in a 1950s "we just won the war, everything's hunky-dory" way should any cars drive by. Using two of us to lift his eyes up level with the bottom of Danielle's second-story bedroom window, making her scream loud enough her dad nearly caught us. Giving Manny Sharpie tattoos and then Windexing them off, making them bigger, louder, worse and better at the same time. Carrying his head into Kroger and hiding him open-eyed in the cantaloupes, running off with him like a football before any clerks or bag boys could catch us. Leaving him on benches in the park and then hiding in the bushes, blowing dog whistles as hard as we could so the dogs would try to attack him, the owners desperately apologizing, trying hard to drag their crazy dogs back to the normal world.

Manny was good for it all, was always game.

Until we kind of just left him behind like a baseball glove we didn't need anymore. Like a tricycle we'd outgrown. Like a friend we'd decided we didn't need to talk to anymore.

I can still see his hand lifted in pre-wave, though. Just waiting for someone to drive by, notice him.

We deserved him coming for us, yeah.

I'm just sorry it had to start with Shanna, who wasn't even in on the prank.

But if Manny'd started with *me*, then a whole lot more people would have ended up dead, so, yeah, sorry, Shanna. Guess it sort of had to be like this. The greatest good, all that, which is also just a way of saying the least bad, which, I know, a truck running off the service road and through your window at sixty miles per hour, that's pretty bad, right?

But yeah, I could have maybe called to warn you, sure. Probably I even should have. And okay, I *didn't* have it all figured out so much yet then, but, I mean, I could have told you about that rattling I was hearing in my backyard anyway. Particularly around the shed. The rakes and shovels, the tomato planters my mom always pins so many of her hopes on.

What I didn't tell you was that my dad sent me out there to chase whatever raccoon or dog away, but instead of a raccoon or dog, I saw a flash of Band-Aid-pale skin in the bushes for a moment. My heart nearly stopped. I froze, looked harder, finally cued in to a painted-on eye watching from a break between the bushes.

Manny.

When we'd been posing him here and there and everywhere, he'd always been stiff, hard to make do what we needed him to.

The level his eye was at now, though, I had to imagine the rest of him crouched down like at the starting blocks for a race. Meaning his fingertips, which had always been more like the front edge of a paddle, had to be holding him up, had to be able to spread wide enough to do that. And his feet would have to be a body length behind him almost, ready to blast him up and away from getting caught doing whatever he was doing.

Was he trembling from the effort of holding this awkward position? Was that trembling making the front half of one of his thighs start to calve off, the dowel in there at just the right angle to slip? Was he still wearing our dads' cast-off clothes or was he naked now, which doesn't really matter for him?

Was he happy to see me?

I was still thinking that, then.

So, yeah, after walking out of the theater like a normal human person, he'd—he hadn't had anywhere to go, anywhere to be, so he'd gone feral, right? Maybe he'd lived on the golf course for a few nights, then remembered where our old fort was back in the trees and gone there, hoping to find us still being kids, still ready to play, still ready for more and more hilarity. But he had to be just operating on dim memories, I figured. And those memories had brought him here, to my backyard, so he could sneak into the garage, maybe. So he could ride away on my dad's Kawasaki, save us the trouble of having to deal with the guilt of him always standing out there at the edge of things. That's the kind of guy Manny would have been, I mean, if he could have been human.

I couldn't leave the garage open for him, though. Even if he could get my dad's motorcycle started, he wouldn't know how to ride it, not really. He'd lay it over the same as my dad had, and his limbs and head and body would go spilling every which way, and *I'd* get busted for it, of course, because he couldn't have done this himself, he's just a *thing*, Sawyer, try telling the truth for once, why don't you?

All the same, I couldn't let him starve, could I?

I whispered to him to wait, then went inside, scavenged for what I imagined a mannequin might eat. It turned out to be bubble wrap and packing peanuts and mayonnaise.

I walked two steps past the light in the backyard, my heart pounding, dropped it all and ran, then came back thirty minutes later to tear the corners off the mayonnaise packets.

The next morning it was all still there, but it was scattered and smeared around, like Manny had looked in this junk for the food part, not found it. But the shed door was swinging back and forth in the breeze, and it had definitely been shut the night before. For absolute sure, because if it wasn't, the raccoons were always out there in their black masks, waiting.

I tiptoed in, saying Manny's name not really hopefully, but like a shield, I guess. Like reminding him I'd known him, once upon a time.

He wasn't there, but my mom's jumbo bag of generic Miracle-Gro had its side ripped open in the most obscene way, most of its pellets not spilling out, just plain *gone*. As many of them that slick plastic fingers would have been able to get out, anyway.

"You eat *that*?" I said out loud to him.

"Eat what?" my dad said back, standing in the open doorway right behind me, then, before I could answer, he asked if I'd seen his Redskins cap, and my traitor of a brain kicked up the rakish angle he usually wore it at, and then suddenly knew why I'd put it at that angle on Manny.

"Maybe Mom put it in the dishwasher again," I told him without looking, and that was enough, he faded like dads do, leaving me with this plundered bag.

"You're growing, aren't you?" I said to the idea of Manny.

The idea of him nodded back.

He was hungry, he was growing, *and* he sort of remembered us.

That combination left me feeling a certain kind of uneasy. A suspicious, dready sort of uneasy.

And then that Mack truck veered off the road into Shanna's room. Unrelated, right?

Wrong.

Because her login was still on my old laptop, I spidered over to her account to see what she'd been pirating the night those headlights came through her window. My idea, I guess, was that if the download had been interrupted, I could finish it for her, at least give her that much closure.

It had been the same superhero movie we'd taken Manny to. I guess—I guess, working there, she only ever saw the credits and the after-scene, right? And, since we'd all watched the first two together so many times, now that she was shut off from us, pissed at us like she should have been, she could still sort of hang out with us by watching the third movie. Or maybe she just wanted to see it, yeah. Mom's right, I always do make things more complicated, see motivations and agendas where there's not much of anything.

Still, *this* movie?

"No, no, *no*," I said, and shut my laptop, held it down with my hand like the truth was trying to rise up, force itself on me.

That it was *that* movie downloading, it told me all I needed to know about how the world was working.

What had happened was some trucker had been lollygagging down the road half-asleep—"lollygag" is my dad's second-favorite word, and his favorite for his first son—but that trucker had been just driving half-asleep like they do, zombies of the highway, and he'd taken the exit without even registering he was leaving the interstate, and then something that had been crouched down on the road in front of him stood up all at once: a mannequin juiced on Miracle-Gro, grown up to sixteen or eighteen feet tall, probably. Maybe twenty. Anybody would have swerved away from hitting a walking nightmare like that, wouldn't they?

Shanna was surely already dead by the time Manny stood up into those headlights, though. He had killed her somehow, probably just strangled her with his plastic hands, then directed the truck through her wall to cover his tracks. That was why they hadn't been able to properly tell what smear of meat was her, what was her mom, which was her little brother, what was dog and what was human.

It had to be like that, though, for Manny.

Otherwise we might clue in that he was coming for us.

He didn't count on me, though.

5

IF SHANNA'S MOM and little brother hadn't died moments after her, *with* her, mixed in together with her—I guess you could say "because of her"—then maybe I would have let things take their natural course. Manny could have just waltzed in—my dad likes that one, too—he could have waltzed in in his stooped-over, giant way and strangled Danielle, decapitated JR, burned Tim, and, I don't know, drowned me in the tiny-to-him toilet like I deserved for dreaming up that prank in the first place.

We all kind of deserved it, I mean.

I'd read *Frankenstein* in AP English, so I knew you don't just walk away from your creations. Not without consequences.

And, to be clear, I was sort of making that up for Danielle and JR about not having been the one that put Manny on my dad's motorcycle. I'd completely put him there, specifically to freak my mom out, make her drop the eggs or something equally hilarious. My dad left him there probably because it felt like at least *some*one was getting some use out of the bike he couldn't ride anymore but also didn't have the heart to sell.

My case for Danielle and JR had been more convincing if I *hadn't* done that, though. I probably learned it from my mom, even, using Miracle-Gro to cheat her garden bigger. That's all lying about Manny on the motorcycle was: Miracle-Gro, to get this idea to bloom up in Danielle's and JR's heads faster.

And it had still been a joke then anyway, right?

It was. Hundred percent.

Sure, Shanna was getting fired and on permanent lockdown, Tim was getting grounded until he grew a pair—*his* dad's go-to—until he grew a pair and quit being a follower, and the prank hadn't exactly shamed the assistant manager like I'd meant, but still, it wasn't a total loss. We had the story of what almost was, didn't we? That's worth nearly as much, if you tell it right.

Anyway, big surprise, before too long there were flyers stapled to every utility pole in the neighborhood. Evidently some deviants of one brand or another were breaking into everyone's toolsheds and gardening supplies, making off with fertilizer, and probably—the word I kept hearing whispered was "surely"—*surely* selling it from the beds of pickups in shady parking lots. Just, evidently, in different bags, because it was never the whole bag of Miracle-Gro that was gone, but just the Miracle-

Gro itself, scooped out the hole torn in the bag's wide, vulnerable belly.

Who would have ever guessed that's what mannequins out in the wild eat, though, right? I mean, who ever even knew there *was* a "wild" for mannequins, but if there is, then: garden fertilizer?

Still, some of that Miracle-Gro, probably most of it, it wasn't only dirt minerals and plant vitamins. Our neighborhood is competitive, I'm saying. Same way Olympic athletes might resort to steroids if they think they can get away with it, a lot of our neighbors, my mom most definitely included, had been opting for the least eco-friendly, closest-to-radioactive grow-fast stuff they could buy. And, the thing was, they *knew* it was dangerous to play with, worse to ever consider actually *eating*. How I knew that? One or the other of the neighborhood SUVs was always pulled over at a farm stand to buy some organic vegetables, the kind that *wouldn't* turn their families into instant mutants.

So, Manny, I had to imagine, from eating that every night for two weeks, he had to be three or four times taller than he'd been for that truck driver, by now. Meaning? He was a *kaiju*, pretty much. The mannequin version of Godzilla. And, being that massive, that towering, that scary, the only place he could hide anymore would be Lake Ray Hubbard, which, tellingly, *was* three or four feet fuller than usual, full enough it was flooding some of the close houses.

I'm not in AP math, so I can't do the numbers for how much water a fifty-foot-tall mannequin would displace, and then factor that into the grade or whatever of the slope around the lake over here on the Rockwall side, but if I could, I know they'd match up perfect.

Manny had to be *giant* by now.

And, in his dim, slow-thinking way, he still had the four of us in mind—four because he didn't have to think about Shanna anymore.

For all I knew, he was even like Frankenstein's monster, right? Maybe he hadn't killed Shanna on purpose, had just been trying to, I don't know, hug her. Maybe he'd just been so happy to see her again after all these years. But we're so fragile compared to a monster like him. He doesn't know his own strength. He just knows he's lonely, and probably afraid. And he doesn't care *what* moms or dads or little brothers or sisters are in the way of him not being lonely, he's just scared without anybody to play with.

Or?

He hates us.

He remembers everything in perfect detail, he's been watching us walk back and forth through my garage for the last three years, never giving our old best friend a second glance.

Either way, we were dead.

Really, I figured, it would be better for the world if we all just killed ourselves. Except of course that would break our parents' hearts and set bad examples for our little brothers and sisters, and everybody at school would have to go to endless assemblies about what to do if you get invited to participate in a group suicide, and we didn't want to be remembered like that. It's much better to be on the murder victim wall, right? The Died Too Young wall?

And, I say "we" here, yeah, because I assume that to be the case, but, I mean, Tim still wasn't supposed to be talking to us, and when I tried to conscript JR in using the vaguest possible outline of "Manny is a giant who's after us," so we could go to Danielle as a *team*, he kept asking if this was a joke or from a movie or what. Meanwhile, Danielle had just, for reasons un-understandable to anyone remotely sane or with an ounce of taste or self-respect, started hard-core dating *Steve* from her yearbook team, so that pretty much just left me to stop the big mannequin killing spree, didn't it?

Sawyer, the only one who figured it out. The only one who knew it was okay if Manny came for us, but it would be way uncool if he also killed our families.

It's kind of heroic, really.

Not that it felt that way.

Tim was first.

6

WHAT I DID TO get ready for what I had to do was download *not* the movie we'd sneaked Manny into—that server pinging would be asking Manny to come kill my family—but one of the earlier ones in the series. I even legit-rented it the day before, left its three-hour ass playing on my laptop so it would go over right before the rental expired, so long as our router didn't reset. Translation: I was home the whole time, trying to stream that movie into my eyeholes before it went away. I'd have to be a crazy person to rent it and not watch it, wouldn't I? Especially with the deadline on it only three hours away, and me getting warnings every few minutes that I was wasting my gift card?

My dad would probably even defend me, if it came to that. It's important to reinforce responsible behavior. Never mind that we have the same movie on DVD in the living room, which was his purchase, so we could bond over the action scenes or learn from the upstanding values or pretend not to be eyeballing the skintight costumes or whatever. What would be important was the "responsible behavior" part of it, this being the "first time in recorded history"—*my* phrase, which he stole, and has been using against me—this being the first time I'd ever exhibited such unteenagerly behavior.

So, my cover was in place. My alibi was streaming in my bedroom, which I wasn't in.

The next part hurt, hurt like you wouldn't believe, chipped an actual piece off my soul I'm pretty sure, then made me swallow it, but it was for the best.

Thing was, not like this is news, but Tim, in addition to his big sister just off to college, he had two little brothers, right? Not to mention a mom and dad who were mostly not terrible, who *should* have grounded him for making them come collect him at the movie theater on their date night. Like all of our families, though, they were potential collateral damage, innocent parties Manny would crush when he reached down through their roof for the kid he used to play with, the kid who used to love him.

And of course we'd all held Tim's little brothers when they were twin babies, held them under supervision, and his mom had chaperoned our bowling parties and museum visits, video'd our recitals, and his dad, I guess he'd never done anything super great, but he did have some old car in their garage he was always saying him and Tim were going to fix up one weekend. It was much more than a weekend job, was more of a "get a different car" kind of thing, but, with dads, sometimes it's the thought that counts, and his dad for sure had a lot of thoughts. Tim's big sister might get out alive when Manny came calling, but that'd just be because she was living in a dorm up in Denton. But who knows, maybe Manny comes knocking when she's home doing laundry, right?

So, like I say, I'm not some AP math whiz, but even I can see that one dead sophomore is so much better than a whole family. It might even make the four of them left, like, bond together more, watch out closer for each other, take more trips. Tim's dad, ex-dad, former dad, grieving dad, whatever, he might even take the twins out to the garage, to work on that hopeless car.

Thing was, though, since I was the only one who'd figured out the path Manny was churning through what had been our group of pranksters, that meant it fell to me to do something about it. Warning Tim would do no good. I *could* reach him, could find out what game he was logged into and chat him up, but what would I say? "Hey, Tim, Manny's been eating my mom's fertilizer, man, and if you want to save your family, you maybe'd better, like, hang yourself in the closet or something, cool? You with me on this?"

His first question back would probably be along the lines of "why *me*," as in, Why *just* him, as in: Why not you too, Sawyer?

He'd be right. People being politely asked to kill themselves have lots of very good, on-point questions. I'd have to explain that it would be me, it should be me, it was going to be me, but for now I was the one saving everybody. My time was most definitely coming, though. If I wanted my family to live through this, then I could no longer be just an *eventual* victim. But first I had to rush around, get things done, save everybody's families until Manny didn't have anybody left to kill, and would have to back off.

And, anyway, I mean—Tim's mom finding him hanging by the neck in his own closet? Really? That would break her heart, would probably destroy the family just as much, only slower. Running away couldn't be an answer either. From Manny's height, he would see us scrambling over county lines, start striding that way, stepping on whoever, it wouldn't matter to him. Then it wouldn't be only our families dying, but completely uninvolved families, times ten, times twenty. And then the air force would probably get involved, and Rockwall, Texas, would be this big national incident blowing up on the evening news.

No, this had to be me. I had to toughen up, like my dad was always telling me.

You were right, Dad.

Thanks for the advice, man.

7

SO, WITH THAT MOVIE playing on my laptop, the garage door still up like I'd "accidentally" left it after dinner, the overhead light long since cycled off, I cleared a path in front of my dad's heavy old Kawasaki, rolled it out to the curb, swung a leg into the creaky saddle, and let gravity and the long slope down to Wilshire take us, popped the clutch at the very end.

When the engine caught, the motorcycle's thready headlight kicked on, its beam shining into the ditch, courtesy of my dad's big wreck. I reached over, straightened the headlight back to center, then followed it. The pegs and bar on the right side were bent up and jagged, the foot brake over there ground half off, the twist throttle catchy, but JR had a dirt bike we'd all lived on freshman year, out at his place. After riding it into the ground a hundred times each, a beaten-up street bike was gravy, was cake, was the most docile pony.

I cut the engine just down from Tim's house, coasted into the trees, tensed up because, with the headlight *off* for this final approach, I might be about to get sliced in half by a barbwire strand I wouldn't see until too late.

Five minutes later I stepped through the sliding glass door of the second side of the garage his dad had converted into an insulated room for his pool table, just, he'd spent so much releveling the concrete floor that there hadn't been any money left over to Craigslist what he was leveling the floor *for*.

The door from the garage to the house was locked, but the key was down a ceramic frog's throat on the other side of the room. I apologized to the frog for making it party to this. In my head I was thinking that the frog thought it was a watchdog, that it had kept Tim's family safe all these years. And if mannequins can walk and talk, then why not, right?

Two creeping minutes after that mumbled apology, I was standing over Tim's sleeping form in the bedroom I still called his big sister's, since he'd just moved into it. He'd fallen asleep in the office chair at his desk, his soldier on-screen caught in a loop of respawning, since this was a hacked game, one he could never lose.

Moving slowly, zero noise, I sidled in alongside him, reached past like I was his third arm, and got his character out of that loop, but still, when I leaned up from that, Tim was watching me with sleepy eyes, like I was maybe a dream.

"Saw?" he creaked, stretching it into a yawn, and of

all the moments of this whole thing, this was by far the longest one. It was like the world was suddenly this huge balloon inflating around me, everything swelling at once, the pressure all around pounding in breath by breath. I hadn't expected him to say my name, I mean, hadn't expected him to call me what he and no one else had been calling me since third grade. I hadn't expected him to not even flinch from me suddenly being there in his room, in my long-sleeved black undershirt from skiing, my mom's black balaclava on my head, my hands in black leather gloves even though it was hot, which should have told him everything he needed to know about my plans.

My eyes maybe got a certain shine to them here, my voice a kind of quaver, my chest a cold hollowness I'd never really known before.

It's not easy, killing your best friend. One of them, anyway.

But, I told myself, this was the only way to save his family from Manny. It was for the best. There was no other choice. If he could, if he knew, he'd tell me to get on with it already.

"I'm sorry for this, T-man," I said to him, and stepped around behind him, a hard loop of light strung from hand to hand, pulling tight around his neck, right where spies in the movies always do it, like the windpipe has vertebra, and what you have to do is slip between two of them.

The line was the glow-in-the-dark filament or cord or whatever you call it from the new edger my dad wouldn't let me use yet. The glow-in-the-darkness was complete stupidity, because who edges at night, everybody would complain about the sound, but still, the one my dad had bought had been the last one on the rack, and it came with a pair of safety glasses tinted in some way that made the glow string really pop, so you could get that edge right where you wanted it.

As for that spool of glowing string, it's like fishing line times a hundred, will only break from slapping into the edge of concrete ten thousand times at high speed. I leaned back on it, each end already looped into junked joysticks because I knew the line would slip from my gloves otherwise.

Tim fell back into me, away from being choked, and I set my feet, let him kick his desk, which dislodged his mouse, switched tabs on his screen and started the video he'd had ready behind the game, for after he made the next level and could stop.

It was the movie we'd taken Manny to. The same one Shanna had been pirating.

I slacked off the line a bit, said without thinking, "Why—why *this* one?"

He just pulled at the line with his fingers, pulled like if I'd let go please he could maybe explain why this movie tonight, but I was in too far to stop now, couldn't let him get enough breath to answer me, because then I might not start in again. But then he did kind of answer. He scrabbled in his pants pocket, kicking to get the angle right, and pulled up that torn ticket stub he hadn't been able to find the night of the prank. Like showing it to me now meant "admit one," I guess? And it kind of did. He had paid for the movie, so downloading it now was just finally using his ticket, was hardly even illegal. But still. I wasn't an usher, right? I didn't have a flashlight to cup in my hand, make his ticket stub real. I was something completely different.

I squinted my eyes in pain with him and pulled back harder, let him scrabble at his neck, at his breathing passages that weren't passing air anymore, his fingernails going deep enough to scratch bright red blood up, the ticket stub fluttering down to rest on the toe of my right shoe.

In the reflection of his monitor I could see his face, dying, and my balaclava'd eyes above, crying.

"I love you, I love you," I said to him during his last few kicks, because I didn't want him to die any more scared than he had to. My shoulders were shaking, my forearms burning, and if I hadn't worn gloves, my hands would have been bleeding, leaving every kind of evidence.

Finally he slumped over, and this was the part I hadn't been expecting, the part the spy movies never go into.

His muscles, without blood flowing through them anymore, I guess, keeping everything in there slick and lubricated, they went kind of instantly creaky, if that makes sense. I could feel them rubbing against each other, I mean, rubbing against each other in a way I could tell was going to lock into place in a few minutes, once the blood pooled in his lower extremities like in all the CSI shows.

I let go fast and pushed away, suddenly sure that creaking-inside feel was going to rush up from him, get into my muscles, leave me dying as well, or at least kill some important part of me. But I guess it kind of did anyway. I fell back onto his bed, cried the rest of my insides out, almost throwing up from it, then rose, punching his stupid Star Wars pillow, hating Manny for making me do this. *It wasn't my fault,* I wanted to scream. I shouldn't have to feel this, like this. I was the hero here, not the bad guy. I was *saving* lives. The few I had to take shouldn't count against me, shouldn't hurt so much. Not when considered against all the people not dying.

Finally I started just breathing deep and raspy, really heaving air in and out.

When I could, I studied Tim dead in his chair, the superhero movie he'd never seen playing right there in front of him.

Finally, hours too late because I'm not a seasoned criminal, I angled my head up to catch any sounds coming from the rest of the house. This hadn't been a completely quiet thing, right?

He didn't have a dog to bark the alarm, though, and his little brothers slept deep enough to sleepwalk sometimes, and his parents were all the way over on the other side of the house, and Meg, his big sister, was probably at a college party or something, wasn't even thinking of her family, of this house.

I came back to Tim, wiped my eyes with my sleeve.

I couldn't let him look like he'd done this to himself, I knew. I could at least give him that, or not add that on, whatever.

To be sure his mom wouldn't have to carry her son having been this big surprise suicide around with her for the rest of her life, I pulled out the flea market knives I'd brought as backup and used them to pin Tim to the wall like an insect in biology. The hands were easy even if getting him up on my shoulder at the same time wasn't, but evidently the feet are full of bones or something, not at all like frogs. When I couldn't get through, even hammering on the butt of the biggest knife with the heel of one of his winter boots, I just pushed the knives through the extra skin of his ankles, jammed the blade tips into the wall as best as I could. It wasn't structural support or anything, but it had a good enough look, and, with both hands stuck to the wall now, and both feet, no way could

Tim have killed himself. He was a victim. And, if I was going to keep on with this, he was a random victim, a big mystery murder, a death out of the blue just like Shanna.

Kids at school would be talking about him for years. For forever.

"You're welcome, man," I said to him, and touched his chest for probably a long ten-count with my forehead, which felt like a real ritual that mattered, that meant everything, that meant enough, and then I left the way I'd come in, wiping the key shiny clean and tinking it back down the frog's throat.

Ten minutes later I had to push my dad's motorcycle the last twenty yards up to the garage, since I hadn't built up enough speed to coast all the way in.

I would remedy that next time.

I was learning.

8

TWO DAYS LATER I called an emergency meeting of those of us not yet dead.

It wasn't to poison the punch on them or explode some homemade bomb. That would have saved a lot of grief, don't get me wrong, but ... remember about our families? A bunch of kids murdered one by one for no reason anybody knows can pull moms and dads and brothers and sisters *together*, but four kids playing with incendiary devices down on the curving pier or long dock or whatever it is down behind Twisty Treats during what would have been seventh period on a weekday, that was the kind of needless tragedy that could leave them all shell-shocked, looking for vices and addictions and affairs to fill our missing spaces with.

I was the first there, but I just watched from the trees in the park, so JR was actually more first.

I wanted to see if he could feel anything from the water, from where Manny had to be sleeping. I wanted to see if the lake would slosh even higher up the shore, from if Manny was sensing a disturbance in the force.

JR just peeled up splinters from the boards at the very end of the dock and threw them like wingless paper airplanes out into the water. Or maybe like little pretend spears, I don't know. He might have been able to see flies or gnats I couldn't make out from where I was.

Did he look like a guy who had just lost two of his lifelong best friends?

I wasn't sure.

Did I look like that?

I touched my face, couldn't feel my fingertips on my cheeks, on my lips, realized I was still wearing the mannequin mask I'd bought earlier at the dollar store. It was just a blank, Band-Aid-colored face, didn't even match my neck skin, my big ears.

I'd bought it for two reasons. The first was that, when Tim had seen me, seen my actual me-face, I'd nearly lost it, nearly quit, nearly had to run away. Second, if I looked like Manny, and if I was doing this *because* of Manny, then it was really like I wasn't even doing it, right? It was like Manny was here himself by proxy, me as his mini-avatar, who could fit into the tight, human-sized spaces. Like this, I was an extension of him, doing what he was going to do, just, not taking out half the school to get it done, not flattening a whole church bus or family reunion or funeral.

But the funerals aren't yet.

And I hadn't meant to leave the mask on for this big meetup, must have forgot I was wearing it.

I took it off like you take a contact out, grabbing the whole thing at once and both lowering my hand and pulling my head back at the same time, to break the seal as gently and painlessly as possible.

My face behind it wasn't even sweating or anything, and my hand wasn't shaking the way it felt it was.

What I looked up to was the flurry of whatever JR was doing down at the end of the dock.

He'd taken his right shoe off, had it hauled back like a baseball from centerfield.

I stepped ahead fast, alarmed, and he sailed it out into the lake.

It floated for maybe ten seconds there, like not sure what to do, like asking was this all right, was this on purpose, did anybody maybe want to take this particular action back, but then it took enough water into its padding and tongue that it had to dunk under, gulp down with a hungry bubble.

JR screamed after it like he was mad at it, then he was hopping, taking his other shoe off. It made him fall down on his ass and he nearly rolled off into the water, but he never stopped pulling on that shoe, finally got it off, threw it like it was on fire, or crawling with red ants.

Next was his shirt, and his belt, and then he was

stepping out of his pants.

When he threw them they unballed in the air, caught some air and fluttered back, snagging on the side of the dock, one leg wet, one hanging on. He ran to that dry leg like he hated it, lay down to push the pants away, away. Probably somebody driving past on the bridge looked over and then looked over again, to be sure what they were seeing was really happening.

"What stage of grief is this?" a voice said from right directly over my left shoulder, practically in my ear.

Somehow I didn't flinch, just looked around.

Danielle.

Without drawing any attention to it, I pressed the back side of the mannequin mask harder to the front of my thigh, said a prayer that JR, stripped down and crying in a very public place, would be more eye-grabby than anything I might or might not be holding.

"The *third* stage?" another voice said, and I turned around to it faster, already grimacing because I'd recognized that cocky, Danielle-kissing voice.

Steve.

He tossed his chin up at me in hey, as if we'd been doing this for years in the halls of all the schools we'd both gone to.

I drilled my eyes into Danielle and she shrugged in a way that told me she didn't have to explain to me about who she chose to bring to our meetings.

It's probably best we were all dying, right? We were falling apart anyway. Too much was changing.

I looked out to JR with her.

"It's the stupid stage of grief," I said, kind of stating the obvious.

"Sounds like somebody's scared," Danielle said back, and I felt more than saw—though I definitely saw, too—her blue button-up shirt peeling up over her head, the two cups of her lime green bra flashing fast in the sunlight.

"All passengers keep their eyes in their heads . . ." Steve drooled out special for my ears only, and then jerked forward because evidently Danielle had his hand, was pulling him with her to the dock, her shirt trailing from her other hand.

On the way, Steve kicked out of his shoes—they were good ones, expensive—and, halfway up the dock, Danielle somehow kept in motion *and* managed to wriggle out of her jeans.

Right when JR turned around, hearing them, she tackled him back into the water.

Steve had to sit down to get out of his socks and pants. He stood in his boxer briefs, looked back to me.

"It's a sad day," he called back. "Anything goes, man." And then he pushed over the side, careful not to snag his underwear on the splinters, and went under with hardly a slurp.

I looked past him, past all of them, to the center of the lake.

Just before Manny surfaced, I knew, there would be a slow bulge out there, like a giant bubble that had been rising for years, was finally, in its ungainly way, coming up to the surface to taste the sky.

I shook my head no about this ridiculousness but pulled my shirt over my head all the same, careful to let the mask stay inside it, and then I stepped out into the sunlight to take my pants off one slow foot at a time, so Steve couldn't say anything about me playing chicken.

To *prove* I wasn't, I stepped out of my underwear as well.

"What the hell is that!" I yelled then, coming up onto my toes to see past them, to the Ferris wheel or wind-turbine blade or whatever that wasn't *actually* coming across the bridge.

When they jerked their heads around to see, I ran for the dock, was in the air by the time they turned back around, cannonballing them before they could think about breathing in, and like that, even with Steve there, it was like all of our summers before, like one last gasp before we went under for good. We splashed each other and sputtered and dove for each other's feet, and—I guess this is why we were doing this—we even smiled some, kind of on accident, and came as high up as we could to wave at the mom pushing her baby stroller past. With two of your lifelong friends dead, that kind of stuff's all you're really looking for, I guess. A moment or two where you forget about being sad.

When we walked up onto shore a few minutes later—no cops there yet, but they always show up eventually if you swim here—when we sat up on the hot pebbly flatness of the water spout hugging our knees, that was when I started crying. Not JR, not Danielle, *me,* who had seen Tim dead before his parents, even. Who had had the longest of anybody to deal with it, had the least reason to be losing it. But I guess I was crying for everything I still had left to do, too. Every*one.* Swimming with them and then drying out with them, it was the best I could have asked for, but it was also the worst thing I could have done.

I stretched my chin up, trying to get loose, get control, and then turned away from them, kind of like to see all the way back to our neighborhoods.

The cops probably weren't here harassing us because, right now, according to all the hushed telephone calls, they were poring over Tim's online interactions to find out if he'd been talking to some internet predator, some drug dealer, some catfisher. When they'd asked me who might have had it out for him, I'd shrugged, licked my dry lips, my chin the stupidest prune of a traitor, and then shook my head no, said it was nothing, it couldn't be him.

Every flip notebook in the room stretched out the spaces between its ruled lines, waiting to clamp shut on whatever I said next.

"It was just a prank," I said, snuffling my nose.

"A prank?" the detective said.

There must be some homicide detective seminar where, for six hours, working in small groups and running drills, they learn to always repeat the last thing the interogee said. Just, put a question mark on it, yeah? *All right now, one more time, we're going to get this right before we leave here today.*

I told them about Manny and the superhero movie, told them all of it, even how Manny was gone when the lights came up.

Was it my way of asking the authorities for help, or was it a smuggled-in confession, some big plea for them to step in, stop me? Either way, they stopped asking me questions and, we all heard later, went and broke up the assistant manager's court-mandated Sunday with his son. Which I feel a little bit guilty about, sure. But it's not like he'd had to be such a dick to us, either.

Really? If he doesn't come down so hard on Shanna, then we never play the big Manny prank, Manny never wakes up, eats fertilizer, kaijus out, and I don't have to . . . well, I don't have to do everything I've had to do, right? I don't have to have all the things in my head that I can't really stop thinking about, no matter how much I hum in my throat.

Anyway, there I am crying on the shore of the lake.

Steve reached his hand for my shoulder but I shook him off, turned away. Evidently there were some coded messages sent through meaningful glances behind my back or over my head, I don't know, but about a minute later he was crunching away, gone.

Now it was me and Danielle and JR, like it should have been.

When JR leaned over to bump me with his shoulder I bumped him back.

"I can't believe he's gone either," Danielle said, rubbing the underside of her left eye with the side of the blade her hand was, which is how girls do it when they . . . don't want to mess up their makeup? When they don't want wrinkles? I don't know. It's not like the lake hadn't already melted her eyeliner and whatever. And it's not like aging was going to be a concern for her either.

"Shanna's gone, too," I said, and JR nodded.

His shirt was washing closer and closer to shore. We all watched it.

"Did you hear it was a devil-thing?" Danielle said to us both.

JR Jesus'd one hand up like against a wall, a knife through the wrist, then he slapped his other hand up, held it there.

"Poor taste, J-man," Danielle said.

"Tim would have done it himself if he were here," JR said.

He was right. What better way to honor him?

"Who was it who, you know," I said, edging into it, watching both their eyes at once, "*found* him?"

"Draco," Danielle spat out, like pissed about the injustice of this.

Draco is what everybody's been calling Tim's little brother Drake since his Harry Potter phase. His twin's Luca, but everybody calls him Luke.

I nodded about this news, taking it in stride.

So the little brother I'd been trying to protect, he was scarred for life now. Great.

He was alive to *be* scarred, though, I told myself.

"Who would do that?" JR said to us both.

"And *why*," I threw in, stealing snapshots of their faces to clock whether my voice was ringing true enough or not.

"He was just Tim," Danielle said, her eyes misting up now.

"And she was just Shanna," I added, getting suspicious

I was maybe the only one who remembered her.

"She was an accident though," JR said.

Her funeral wasn't tomorrow because, so the scuttle-butt said, they hadn't been able to rake enough of her up to be sure what was her, what was the two Rottweilers that famously slept on the bed with her.

"Dead's dead," Danielle said, and I nodded with that, couldn't stop nodding.

Already, sick as I know it is, already, sitting there with them in some made-up stage of grief called "skinny-dipping," I was ping-ponging my eyes back and forth between them a little, trying to decide who next.

It doesn't mean I'm a good friend.

What I was weighing, it was if it's better to be one of two left, or to never have to get to that stage, where it's feeling inevitable, where you're seeing a blade around every corner, teeth in every shadow.

"His service is Wednesday," Danielle stated, just a fact.

"Isn't he evidence?" I asked. "Don't they need to, like, keep him until they have a suspect or whatever?"

Danielle looked at me like the weirdo I probably sounded like.

"Watch *SVU* much?" JR said, half his mouth smiling.

"I bet I know what he was watching," I said then, laying it out there.

They both looked to me, waiting.

"That team-up movie," Danielle finally said. "One we—we brought *Manny* to?"

"It's already posted?" JR said, incredulous. "It's still in the theaters, isn't it?"

I shrugged.

"Why do you think he was watching it?" Danielle asked, hugging her knees tighter, her chin right on top of them, her hair frizzing all around her.

"I hope he was, I mean," I said, looking back out across the water for a wet bulge slowly crowning up. "I never even got to see it that night, did y'all?"

It was how I was deciding who was next. Whichever of them had, that would be the next victim raising their hand. But neither of them said anything.

We just sat there like a math problem, like the remainder left over after everything's gone to hell.

"I think I'm going to fix up my dad's motorcycle," I said at last.

"I can help," JR said.

"Count me in too," Danielle said, and I pursed my lips in an inside smile, a maybe thankful smile, because nobody lies with better intentions than friends. They each patted me on the shoulder when they left, and Danielle kissed me on the top of the head, and somehow I didn't catch on fire from all the heat and anger and sadness swirling inside me.

I just kept staring across the lake.

9

OVER DINNER THE NIGHT I was to kill Danielle, my dad told a wandering-all-over story about *his* dad taking him fishing. He basically has two fishing stories: one is the time a bird dive-bombed the spoon lure he was casting, snagged it in midair, and the other's this one about him and Grandpa sitting out there on top of the lake at dawn, like two versions of the same person balanced on top of this great cliff of water over by the dam, and Grandpa's got this deep-sea rig going on that he'd bought at a pawn-shop. Because that's how you pull up the giant catfish that's supposed to be floating down there like a zeppelin, its whiskers as thick as a man's arm.

Spoiler: they don't catch it this day. Fish stories aren't about what happened, they're about what almost happened, what should have happened, what was so close to actually happening that, in the telling and retelling, it sort of *starts* to happen.

So me and my mom sat through Grandpa feeling a twitch in that thick line, then the line running out, then Dad scooping lake water up onto the reel, and then

Grandpa setting the line, and how it jerked the whole boat forward, as mimed by the dollop of mashed potatoes on the end of my dad's fork.

I think he tells that story because he knows him and me are never going fishing like that, but if I can just feel that rush he felt that day the boat jerked with magic, then it'll sort of be like I was there with them, three generations of us in one tight boat, and like that he's absolved of having to get up at four in the morning, haul us down to the boat ramp.

And, really? That's pretty okay with me.

This time through the story I was just watching how tight that deep-sea fishing line of Grandpa's probably was before it snapped. And how it was probably bright green, and how nobody except me would ever know how that mattered, how that matched up with a certain coil of line in my pocket that I kept having to sneak touches down to, to be sure it hadn't slithered away, to be sure it wasn't going to go killing without me. Another thing I was the only one to be seeing on continual loop, I'm pretty sure, was Shanna, lying in her bed with her two dogs, and how both of them probably popped their heads up right when those Mack headlights flashed her window into a sun.

I hope she wasn't scared, I mean. I hope it was fast.

Like it wasn't with Tim.

But that was my first try. He was practice, he was me finding my feet.

And what I really hated at the same time I was kind of looking forward to it was that, for Danielle, I was probably going to be better—stronger, faster, less hesitation. I liked it for her, of course, I didn't like to think about her suffering and being scared, but a thing like I was about to have to do, it *should* be hard for the person having to do it, shouldn't it?

I wasn't sure I *wanted* to get better. I wanted each time to be a barely situation, an it's-not-going-to-work-this-time-I-can't-do-it situation, a skin-of-my-teeth thing that could go either way, at least until luck or fate steps in, decides it so I don't have to.

"Mim lost a whole *chicken*," my mom said then, like the most delicious neighborhood gossip, and I kind of heard it on delay, clawing up out of my own head, back to the dinner table.

"Chicken, hm," my dad said, trying to tease an over-thick slice of bell pepper from his meat loaf and stealthily guide it away from anything on his plate he was maybe planning on eating, him being forever on the team that thinks only meat and breadcrumbs and egg and ketchup go into meat loaf.

"She doesn't have a *chicken*," my little brother Beanie said, perfectly aping my mom's out-loud italics.

"Off her grill, dear," my mom said. "It was . . . she was—what's the word, where you spin it like a hot dog?"

"Ferris wheel?" I tried, providing my usual level of help.

"Rotisserie," my dad said sort of with a harrumph, so you could like hear a newspaper page turning loud and crinkly in his hands. Because this is 1950, yeah. But still, I could sort of hear it in his impatient, kind of disgusted delivery.

"And Dave and LouAnne on the corner," my mom went on, leaning in and raising her eyebrows because we were so supposed to call bullshit on this, "she was unloading her groceries, and she says one of her bags went completely missing. Just, boop, gone!"

"She's the one who can't keep up with her dog?" my dad asked.

"Bags of groceries don't chase after squirrels, dear," my mom said back to him.

"Just saying," he said.

"Somebody's stealing this stuff?" I couldn't help asking out loud. "Like—like, whoever was getting the fertilizer or whatever?"

"Oh, oh," my mom said, the underside of her fingers to my dad's forearm, for his full attention, "if we file a police report, homeowner's will cover however many bags we say we lost. *However* many."

"Wasn't me," Beanie said in his chipper, guilty way, and I considered him and his third-grade self for a moment, trying to figure if he could have been responsible for the rash of nocturnal Miracle-Gro thieveries, if he and his friends could be the ones stealing groceries and opening up backyard barbecue grills like presents.

No, I decided. No way.

But did that leave Manny, then? Why would a man made of plastic want human food? And why would he want so little? For his appetite, at the size he was now, he'd have to stride out past the city limits, scoop up a whole herd of cattle, chase them down with a handful of horses.

More important, how could he sneak into a backyard, open a barbecue? He'd have either ripped the top completely off the grill, or he'd have left some of his melted plastic on the heated-up outside. Either way, Mim would have felt her house falling into a great shadow or something, wouldn't she have? The streetlights probably would have even come on, with Manny all between them and the sun.

No, it didn't make sense.

And LouAnne on the corner, my dad was right, she was always losing something. Her bag of groceries was probably in the parking lot down at the store.

So maybe it *was* Beanie and his buds, I told myself.

We'd have done the same thing ourselves back then,

if we'd have thought of it. Not for the chicken, but just to get away with it. Just for how wide you smile, running away.

"She probably lost it into that sinkhole," my dad offered, trying to send this discussion down after LouAnne's groceries. To him, I guess, if it didn't involve giant catfish, it didn't notch high enough to warrant dinner conversation.

"Sinkhole" opened a whole nother can of worms, though, at least for me. Very interesting worms.

"A . . . *what*?" I said, drawing my mom's hand/mouth motion that I know means I'm not supposed to speak with my mouth full.

My dad darted his eyes up like caught actually saying something interesting, and then, with deliberate slowness, he forked another bite of mashed potatoes in and savored them, making us wait.

Giving my mom time to cut in, of course.

"Not the one at Katelyn's," she assured me, reaching over to pat the top of my hand like I might be about to explode. Katelyn is her cousin, Shanna's mom. What was wrong with her lawn, okay, what we'd done that ended her up working at the theater to pay her mom back in the first place, I guess starting all of this? We'd had this plan to make slam dunk videos in her driveway with this new steadicam little handheld thing Tim had for his phone.

The idea was he was going to run alongside whoever was dunking, and then fall down and away when we jumped, making it look like we were launching up into the sky. The trick would be keeping the ground out of the frame, so nobody would be able to tell we had Shanna's rim lowered down to eight feet. Anyway, great plan, kind of bulletproof really, we'd have been instant internet stars, would probably get corporate sponsors and movie offers, had the school renamed after us, all that, but . . . when Shanna spirited Aunt K's car keys out from their hook so I could back her Tahoe out of the way, well. We didn't know if putting it on the road was illegal or not out where they live, so I carefully, super carefully backed it over beside the house, did a perfect job of it.

That lasted for about three minutes of dunking, at which point Danielle had said, in her nervous voice, "Guys?"

We looked where she was, at the Tahoe's headlights pointing up at the sky.

The ass-end of the truck was sinking, exactly like it had just got pegged by a meteorite or something.

"Oh, oh," Shanna said, covering her mouth, shaking her head no.

The Tahoe was parked on the septic tank, yeah. One tow truck and a backhoe later, Shanna got the bill and the judgment from her mom, and all of this started.

"That's not a real sinkhole," my dad said. "More of a shi—"

Mom cut him off with just her eyes, which is kind of like a mom-power.

My dad looked down into his plate, came back up looking at me, said, "It's on Oak, you don't have to worry about it."

"A *sinkhole*?" I repeated.

"Right in the middle of the street," Beanie said with a thrill.

"Shaped like a car," my dad added with a shrug, pushing his plate away like he wasn't going to have to carry it to the kitchen himself.

I watched his plate and nodded, kept nodding, envisioning this car-shaped crater one street over.

If scale isn't a thing, then the outline of a car and a giant foot are about the same shape, aren't they?

They are.

I felt my face going numb, my breath coming in deep and cold.

What I was doing was imagining Manny walking down the middle of Oak after midnight, casting his painted-on eyes left and right, looking for the next one of us. Only then he steps down onto a part of the street that crumbles under his massive weight, his foot stabbing down ten, twenty feet, unbalancing him, his great arms wheeling around over the houses, the utility-pole-sized dowels in his thighs threatening to let go, spill him down across two or three roofs.

He gets control though, barely, and hauls his foot up, backs away, ashamed at having broken a people-thing.

Would the crew tasked with fixing this sinkhole find the asphalt at the bottom of the hole not just fallen in, but crushed down? Would they make the necessary connections, draw the good deduction, save me from having to finish what I'd started?

I shook my head no, they wouldn't.

It takes real imagination to connect the dots the right way. Imagination with a little helping of guilt.

"Nothing either of you need to worry about," my mom said to Beanie and me then, about the sinkhole on Oak, maybe saying it because I was shaking my head back and forth real slow. She probably read it as fear, because I was in a delicate state and all, having just lost two friends.

Moms are so oblivious. It's like they live in a bubble of wishful thinking.

Not that my dad really paid enough attention to have to resort to that kind of thinking.

"Well then," he said, balling his paper towel up and depositing it on the table, signaling to us this little interlude was over, thanks for playing. Over for him anyway. Not so much for me.

After dinner and dishes, before I claimed homework and disappeared to my bedroom to crawl out the window, sneak around to the garage, I made sure to corner Beanie away from Mom and Dad.

"What?" he said, trying to wriggle out of my hold on his arms, probably thinking I was about to hold him down to the carpet, dangle another line of spit over his face while he squirmed, me being a big brother and all, him being mostly a twerp.

I came down to his level this time, though, looked at him like an actual person.

"Just—I want to," I started, not sure how to say this because there hadn't been any time to rehearse, "if, like, you and your friends, Gabe and Alexa and whoever, if y'all find a mannequin like from the department store, then you know not to play with it, don't you?"

He stared at me like waiting for the rest of whatever this was going to be.

My idea was that the Miracle-Gro, it had to wear off at some point, so Manny could shrink back down to his original size, get found again, start this whole cycle over.

"It's a trick high schoolers play," I told Beanie, making it up as I went. "They catch all the roaches they can, like from a house that's being gassed, and they cut a hole in the mannequin—"

"Where?" Beanie asked.

"The back of the head," I said, obviously, but also because I know he wanted me to say *butt*, so he could laugh, picturing it. Like I said: third grade. "Anyway, they fill the mannequin up with roaches, right? And then they tape that hole over, then they leave it there for kids to find. They call it a 'roach bomb.' When you move it, bam, roaches all over you."

Beanie's face went slack by bad degrees.

Roaches have always been his terror. Not because they're actually mean or anything, but because they're like dirty bullets with legs, dirty blind bullets always aiming at your feet when you just want to suddenly be able to fly.

"You know what a mannequin is?" I asked then, and he looked away, his eyes kind of wet because me talking about roaches had already gotten him going, I think.

Funny what scares people.

For me, what was a thousand times scarier than a bug was a blank-faced man made of plastic watching a whole movie, then standing *up* from that movie, walking away into the real world.

And also having to stab Tim to his bedroom wall, after choking him with a glow-in-the-dark edging line. And Shanna seeing her bedroom window suddenly bright with headlights.

And thinking about Danielle, later.

You're stalling, I told myself.

It was true.

I rubbed Beanie's hair every which way and pushed him away hard like you do when you can't really hug.

Thirty-eight minutes later, the garage door artfully left up again, I pushed my dad's big Kawasaki out, breaking that dusty red laser sensor that clicked the overhead light on, throwing my shadow down in front of me, all stretched out and evil.

I lowered my head, both hands to the bike's grips, and stepped into it.

10

BECAUSE DANIELLE HAD DOGS the same as Shanna had—just yappers, not killers, but still, *loud* yappers—I had to catch her away from her house.

Which? I guess I was saving her dogs too, right? Manny would stomp on dogs as soon as he would crush a family. Maybe even faster, since they'd be sniping in, trying to bite through the hard plastic shell of his feet, get to the pulpy center they knew had to be in there somewhere.

This is what I do, I save people. And dogs.

Anyway, catching her away from her house meant catching her on a date with Steve, one it felt like they were making up as they went along.

In disguise at the vigil for Tim—hoodie, sunglasses, gloves—I kept two or three car-lengths away from them, which was about eighty or ninety students' worth of padding. Steve was holding Danielle's hand like he owned her, like he was being "strong" for her in this painful, tragic time. The flags in front of the high school were fluttering halfway down the poles like, I don't know, like Tim had been a federal building or something, I guess.

There was crying and swaying and singing, and then this part I hadn't expected, where everybody filed past the school mascot, a cartoon ranger, and left roses and stuffed animals and beer bottles and notes folded over three or four times, held down with rocks.

Tim's family would have loved it, if they'd been there. But, even not there to appreciate all this love Tim was getting, still, they were one hundred percent *alive,* I knew. Hugging each other and crying and not having any answers, but Tim's little brothers, they were going to live, and someday Tim's mom and dad were probably going to be grandparents, and Tim had been going to die *anyway,* so it's not like I even really did anything, right? Anything except save them.

It was like—I was in AP Physics for a couple of weeks, right? Before the math really started? So, in physics, which is also the world, every action has an equal and opposite reaction. Or, that *r*eaction, if you look at it the other way, it has a distinct cause. Them being alive and healthy and grieving and all, that was a *reaction* to the cause I'd been, to me sneaking into Tim's room and killing him.

Just, if I wanted to save everybody else, I couldn't say any of this out loud.

Another way to look at that action/reaction thing, it's that, like that one guy says at the end of the second of those three superhero movies—he's not even a hero, just a hanger-on journalist writing about all this—*Sacrifices must be made.*

In AP English that would be passive voice, which erases agency, hides the actual doer of the thing.

That's how I was saying it in my head the whole vigil, specifically *because* it erased me from the equation: Sacrifices were having to be made. Prices were having to be paid.

Anyway, I held a candle and swayed back and forth and tried to have big meaningful flashbacks like everybody else, always keeping Danielle in sight, and when the wax dripped down onto the web of skin between my thumb and first finger I gritted my teeth and rode the burn out, which is how I knew I had what it took to do this thing all over again.

From the vigil, Steve drove them to the burger place Danielle's always liked, the one across the lake, the one that *I* showed her the double-secret menu for. She ordered off it, I know. I was in the bushes in the parking lot, would definitely get seen if I tried to hunch over in a booth two away from them, but the way she ate her whole burger, then the end of Steve's—yeah, the secret menu. And the way she ate his burger, without cutting around where he'd bit, it was like the most public kiss ever.

I wanted to look away, but I couldn't lose track of them.

On the way to Steve's compact, sensible little hatch-back—of course he'd drive something like that, not any-thing cool and outlaw like a wrecked motorcycle—the whole way to that wimpmobile, Danielle was on the phone with her mom, explaining how she'd be home later, she was still, like, "sad and stuff, okay?"

I don't blame her for that. I mean, she *was* sad, I'm sure, even if she wasn't crying and wailing and messing up her makeup like so many of the girls at the vigil, who'd never had time for Tim when he was alive and it might have mattered.

Then, like the world whispering to me that I was on the right path here, Steve-o drove the two of them over to the worn-out version of the movie theater Shanna had worked at: the dollar show, a four-screener in a mall that still said "Sears" and "JCPenney" and the rest, but in these shadow letters, because the signs had all been taken away, like the world had moved on without this place.

By now, the superhero movie we'd taken Manny to had cycled to places like this, right?

I'd been hesitating, watching them, thinking if Manny came for Danielle while she was out with Steve, and

Steve got crushed in a giant footprint or whatever, that would be no great loss, really. I might even get bonus points.

But, I had to remind myself, if they were on a *date*, then they'd be in a sort-of public place, and there'd be other people getting stepped on, not just Steve-o the raging pube.

I shouldn't call him that, it's from sixth grade and we'd all had individual discussions with the counselor about it, but I've also never been able to stop.

Anyway, a few minutes after the movie started, I paid my dollar-fifty, ducked in after them. Because this isn't the real movie theater, there's no assigned seating, you just find wherever you want, plop down. And because this was all meant to be, because I was doing the right thing, Danielle and Steve weren't in the back row, where they could see any dark shapes slouching up on them. They were in what I guess, if we'd all lived, we might have started calling the Manny Seat: right in the middle of everything.

Scattered around the rest of the theater there were maybe fifteen other couples, all of them not so much paying to see the movie as paying to have nearly three hours to sit in the back so they could grope and fondle and—my mom's gross way of putting it—"pet."

I slunk down the aisle, sat way on the end in the row

behind Danielle and Steve.

While nobody was looking, I slumped down lower and lower, finally palmed my mask up from the hoodie's kangaroo pocket. Part of keeping on with a thing like I was doing, it's leaving no witnesses to describe you. That would just slow you down.

So, I sat through the first hour of the movie again, all the setups and ridiculously obvious payoffs, the CGI overkill, the in-jokes and follow-throughs and tie-ups from the first two installments, and for a few minutes I even forgot what I was doing there, I was just another patron, enjoying the movie as much as it could be enjoyed.

But then, suddenly, Danielle was standing in front of me, staring right at me, the bright movie screen behind her glowing through her hair like *she* was the superhero.

I opened my mouth, waiting for some lie to come out that could place me here, but then it hit me: because the seats are so close front-to-back at the dollar theater, hardly enough room even for knees, not unless you chock them up on the back of the seat in front of you, she was having to turn sideways to shimmy down to the aisle, escape up to the lobby.

For a moment, though, I swear she kind of saw me, saw my eyes behind that mask.

I looked away, grunted something she could maybe hear as *down in front* or *stupid entitled kids*, and then she was past, was gone to the lobby for whatever, probably thinking I'd been an accident victim or something—the mask, the late hour, the lonely place—and should she buy me a bucket of popcorn, or would that be an insult? That's how she thought, trust me. And it made it worse somehow, what I was actually here for. I went cold on the inside, slumped down lower than I already was, like a submarine periscope sinking in a cartoon, and by slow degrees, in complete ninja mode, I crawled down to directly behind Steve, all fixated on the big animated finale on-screen.

Now that Danielle was gone, he could scratch and adjust himself to his heart's content. Enough that it almost seemed like maybe there was more going on, like, in the darkness of the dollar theater, he was making a move on himself.

Like I say, I never went for Steve, not really. And I have zero idea what Danielle saw in him. As proof of his, like, character, or lack of character, who goes to a happyfun good-guys-win superhero movie when his girlfriend just lost one of her best friends in the most violent way? And lost him just a couple of weeks after losing her *other* best friend, who she'd had since first grade?

"Piece of shit," I whispered, and Steve froze, turned his head to the side, probably not sure he'd heard what he'd for sure heard.

My glow-in-the-dark cord whipped up into the dusty projector light like a tentacle in a monster movie, soaking in every last lumen it could, then looped down over his throat, the joystick handle falling perfectly into my waiting hand. Because his chair was bolted to the cement floor—Tim's had been a rolling office chair, a hand-me-down from his dad—this was miles easier, leverage-wise. And because Steve was lanky tall, he couldn't even limber his legs and feet up enough to make a real racket.

He grabbed, pulled, then finally spasmed to death so much faster than Tim had.

I slithered the cord back to me, lay down on my back, waiting, and what I had to become aware of at the level I was at, it was the same thing we'd all had to think of when we'd been snapping Manny back together at the front of the theater for the assistant manager: those senior football players, peeing down the smooth concrete slope of the theater.

The reason I was having to think it this time, and on this side of the lake, it was that, in death, Steve's body had relaxed or whatever, and now *his* pee was dripping down past his seat, was splashing one oily drop at a time onto the concrete right in front of my mannequin face. It rolled the other way, thank gravity, but not until it had pooled up some. The incline or decline or whatever at the dollar show isn't exactly steep, right?

Then—I could only see because that puddle was so close to my eyes—the whole theater, like, *shook,* or rumbled, like an asteroid had just hit in the parking lot. I feel guilty for saying it, but my heart kind of leapt here. That sound, that crushing impact, it could only really be Manny, right? There was no reason he couldn't clamber up from this side of the lake if one of us was over here. And now there were *two* of us over here? He'd probably watched us the whole way across the bridge, Danielle in the passenger seat of a puttering wimpmobile, me on an unmufflered Kawasaki 750 with a shaky headlight. And, if it was him, if he was showing himself before I could finish with our little crew, what that meant was everybody was going to have to understand why I'd been doing what I'd been doing, what I was right now doing—what I'd just *done.* Really, though, compared to the body count Manny was probably about to leave in his wake, the body count and the damage to this condemned mall, Steve-o would probably be completely forgotten, just another body in the rubble. And Tim and Shanna would, in hindsight, just be prelude, prequel, prologue, whatever, which I guess is the way I think from having seen that third installment of the superhero movie so many times by now.

Anyway, as soon as I knew the ground shaking had to be Manny, I also had to think of that sinkhole footprint he'd left on Oak, and how that wasn't the end I wanted for Danielle, seeing a giant smooth foot coming down for her.

"I'm already here!" I screamed as loud as I could, up into the theater at Manny, hoping he could hear through the ceiling, not caring that rest of the moviegoers *definitely* could. "I'm already doing it!" I told him, and I guess everybody. *"You don't have to!"*

After, there wasn't exactly silence, but all the people muttering and standing and wondering, getting gruntled up, they were background static anyway, quiet enough for the shrieking in my head to somehow jump *out* of my head, be all around: the old system of tornado sirens, they were winding up, doing their moany *arooo* thing. Which made sense, since there'd been a warning-crawl on the television at dinner, the whole way through my dad's catfish story, but tornado warnings are every night in Rockwall, at least toward the end of spring semester.

I leaned my head up to hear better, to feel if there was a change in pressure, like some impossible whirlwind was sucking all the air up to the clouds to slam it back down at us, but all there was was hammers and fists through the dollar show's speakers, and one of the superheroes on screen screaming in outrage when she finds that destroyed colony of peaceful aliens.

You can still do this, I told myself.

None of the tornado sirens are ever actually real, or they don't really indicate a tornado, they just get everybody riled up, diving for the basements and shelters. Seriously, in my whole life I've seen one funnel actually touch the ground, and it was way across a field. It maybe killed a mouse or two. I mean, sorry, mice, you matter too, but this was probably going to be another crying-wolf thing, like always.

That didn't keep the house lights from coming on, though.

Worse, what they lit up for me was Danielle, standing at the end of the row, looking down at what the lights had lit up for *her*: me. Or, not "me" exactly, but some guy lying down behind her boyfriend. Some guy who, when he looked up to her, had a mannequin face. Except for the eyes.

She tracked up from me to Steve, his head lolled back over the chair, his eyes probably open and dry, staring up at the ceiling, a raw red line surely circling his neck.

Danielle dropped the coke she'd gone for, was running before it hit the floor.

And, I admit it, I was crying now, sort of, behind my mask. Starting to, just quietly. Not because of Steve, who cares about him, but because, ever since I'd started doing this, I'd accidentally started kind of imagining that when it was over, Danielle was going to wake up, see me for who I really was, and that was going to be the beginning of everything. Never mind that she was on the kill list, that she had to be sacrificed if we hoped to save her family from Manny. It was a dream, all right? A wish, like.

But then that wish, it sort of was coming true already—what she was doing, standing at the end of the row, was finally seeing the real me. Just, it was the one who killed Tim, the one who, as far as she knew, had probably killed Shanna as well.

The one who was coming for her, now that her boyfriend was out of the way.

I slapped a hand to the back of a seat and hauled myself up, didn't let myself think of her mom raising her like she had, her mom working two shifts to pay their bills and whatever, and her little sister doing her hair just like Danielle's but doing it all wrong, and somehow better, in a little-kid way.

You can't let yourself see that kind of stuff when you're about to have to kill that person. And you also can't re-see her running for the shimmery surface of the lake, her shirt falling away behind her, the strap of her bra across her back *black,* not bright green like you'd have expected, to match the cups.

Do the math, do the math, I told myself as reminder, for resolve.

She had *two* family members, where Tim had had four,

five counting his big sister, but still, her mom and sister hadn't done anything to deserve Manny's wrath, had they? And, I mean, who knows, maybe Marcy, her little sister, maybe she's going to grow up to fly to Mars and invent the big space-polio vaccine or something, and her mom's going to watch her on the television, and Marcy's going to say into the mic for all the world that this is for her sister, whom she still misses and thinks about every day.

Her sister who died watching a superhero movie.

I raced to the end of the row, fell out into the aisle, my chest already heaving, my mouth behind the mask gulping all the plastic-tasting air it could.

"I'm sorry, D," I called out to her, and my voice vibrating the thin mask and tickling my lips, the *sound* of my voice, of her best friend's voice, it stopped her.

She turned around, cocked her head over to the side, probably seeing Manny's face and trying to make that track with what she'd just heard.

"Sawyer?" she said, kind of parentheses around her eyes, like her mind was in a holding pattern, was so ready to tell her lips to smile, that this was some big terrible joke.

"This more of a lobby thing than a ruin-the-movie thing, maybe?" some dude said, the question mark not really a question mark, of course.

I let the long loop of glowing green line unspool down from my hand and blinked away the tears forming in my whole body.

Danielle took one step back, bumped into some woman running for the exit, probably sure a tornado was about to drill down into us, or maybe thinking I was some shooter even though I didn't have a gun, and banging into her knocked Danielle hard to the side, her ribs catching the front corner of one of the dollar show's ancient-old wooden armrests.

She folded around it but never stopped watching me, my whole six long steps up to her.

Because I didn't want to scare her anymore, and because I was pretty sure my voice would break anyway, betray me, I came around beyond her, looped the string around her throat, her hair tangled in it, and pulled back hard to make this fast, and the least painful for her as I could. It's what you do for someone you secretly love.

I pulled hard enough that her hair tore and her head popped back, something in there creaking loud and kind of snapping, and then her chin kind of lowered forward onto her chest.

"Danielle?" I was able to say then, kind of a croak, my mask right down by her face now.

Her eyes were still wet, staring, the dark pupils dilating wide from whatever she was seeing now, where she was.

I pushed the mask up onto my forehead and, for the first time, as goodbye, as hello, kissed her slow and soft on the cheek, and touched her lips with the side of my gloved index finger, and then I was flying backward.

My first thought was that I'd waited too late, that Manny had cracked the roof of the theater open, had me pinched between his massive fingers, but then it was some moviegoer infected with superheroism, showing off to his girlfriend or boyfriend or whoever.

He slung me up, my mask catching on Danielle's hair or something and popping back down onto my face mostly lined up, only blocking *most* of my vision, and when he saw me, he flinched back hard, fell back into a row himself, ending up sitting down perfect in the end seat like ready for the movie to continue.

"I'm sorry, I'm sorry," I said, to him, to Danielle, to everyone, and then hit it, running hard for the exit door, diving out and running for the parking lot three empty storefronts down, where my dad's motorcycle was waiting on its kickstand, the sky green above and around me, boiling with murder.

In the special report on the news that night, Blankface was born.

"No," I said, sanding the eyeholes of my mask larger with my mom's emery board. "It's *Manny*."

11

THEY DIDN'T SHUT SCHOOL down for Danielle's and Tim's funerals like they should have—there wasn't enough of Shanna to bury, and, with her family dead, there was nobody to bury her *for*—but they weren't counting absences either.

I don't know whose idea it was to do a double service, but I guess it saved everybody having to find different black dresses and jackets and dark sunglasses for the next time around. This way it could be one-and-done, like my dad used to say when he coached our Little League.

The whole high school and most of the town stood there in the hot wind and listened to the speakers drone on about "too young" and "called home" and whatever, but a lot of people, instead of all-the-way listening, they were watching the clouds build on the horizon. The tornado the alarms had screamed about while Danielle was being killed hadn't actually happened, but around here you never know. At least that's what everybody's always saying. Better safe in the cellar than sorry halfway up into the sky, all that.

Because JR and me were the last ones left, we got to stand right at the very front.

When everybody's looking at you like that, you kind of have to turn your whole face into a mannequin, right? At least I did. Every time I licked my lips, I could see someone out there waiting for me to start crying.

I didn't have any tears left in me, though. The whole night after Danielle, I'd pretty much emptied out, and ever since then all I could think about was that it was almost over. It was almost over except for one person.

Was it fitting that JR would be last? I mean, because it was his creek we'd originally found Manny in. Was it all coming full circle, like teachers and coaches and parents love so much, like it confirms for them that the world makes sense, is following some big design or whatever.

But he wouldn't actually *be* last, I told myself.

If the barber of Spain cuts everybody's hair, who cuts his hair, all that.

I'm the barber, here.

I was making sure everybody else showed up obviously killed, so their parents wouldn't have to live with feeling guilty for their kid having offed him- or herself, but who could give *me* a neck-level haircut at the end of the day, right?

I didn't have everything figured out, no.

I was kind of getting through this on a night-by-night

basis, now. A friend-by-friend basis. I probably wouldn't even get to go to JR's funeral either, I knew. If I tried, everybody would form a ring of bodies around me to keep me safe, right? But that would just get more people crushed when Manny stands up from the lake, brings his big foot down ... maybe not *on* me, but close enough where he thinks he can like lean down, let me crawl up onto his hard plastic palm.

Oh, the fun we'll have then.

That's my sarcastic voice, yes.

When Manny takes you into the lake, you drown in the cage of his hands, I have to think.

We should have left him lying there in JR's creek. We never should have been rolling down that hill in those boxes. We should have been, I don't know, stealing chickens from backyard barbecues. Playing video games, fishing, making out, shooting endangered woodpeckers with BB guns, a hundred other things.

Every time I sneaked a look up at all the mourners watching me, too, I kept expecting one of those faces to be wearing the mannequin mask. I wouldn't think it was Manny—I *knew* where he was, and what size he was—but I would think that whoever was flashing that blank face at me, they'd be doing that because they knew I was faking it, that I was the one responsible for all this.

It seems so obvious when you're the one with blood

on your hands, right? Like everyone's watching you. Like everybody's waiting.

Even if I did get caught, though, then that would still just be one family wrecked, not five. Well, not four, I guess, since Shanna's family *did* get literally wrecked.

I don't want to have to do any more math, please.

I also didn't want to have to do what I knew I had to, to finish this out.

I could see JR's eyes darting around in his mask of grief the same as mine, I mean. I can only imagine how terrifying it must be to know you're for sure in the victim pool but not be able to see the face of the legs walking around and around that pool. The blank plastic face.

I'm sorry, JR, I said to him in my head, standing right there beside him. I really am, man. One hundred percent.

It's just—you're one person, not a whole family. And Manny doesn't care, man. I don't think he's mean, he's just huge and clumsy and lost. In *Frankenstein*—you haven't read that yet, have you?—they never kill the monster there, I mean. He just ends up way up in the Arctic, snow islands floating all around him, like he's going to freeze, right? Just sleep it out till later.

I think that's what Manny's going to do too. Just, he'll do it in the lake.

For all we know, that's what he was doing when he turned up in the slime of that creek, even. For all we know, some covered-wagon kids or some other Indian kids were best friends with him a hundred years ago, and finally left him behind too when they grew up, and he just waited it out. Waited for us.

And, for a while, we were so perfect for him. We were everything to him, weren't we? He was the perfect toy, until he wasn't. Until we started groaning when one of us had dressed him up in some hilarious outfit, left him on somebody else's lawn.

He was always willing, though.

We loved that guy.

And it was probably mean to bring him back for just one prank, I know. If I don't think of that, we're all alive, I mean, we're going to be seniors and graduate and have lives and kids and affairs and everything.

That's why I'm taking it on myself to do what I have to do.

It's not my fault exactly, but it sort of is, too, if you look at it from just one side, like.

Anyway—this is what I was *also* whispering in my head at the funeral, and what I told myself JR had to be whispering the same, right beside me—anyway, I didn't even really want to live if all my friends were dead. Better to be with them than to be without them.

In the inside of my new blazer I had special for the funeral, slid down into the liner I'd cut a secret slit in, was the mannequin mask. Just for in case the adults or whoever decided JR and me needed some time alone, at our old haunts or whatever.

But, no.

The rest of the day there was a crowd of people thronging around us the whole time.

It wasn't until eight days later that I was able to get JR sort of alone.

Except then that all blew up too.

12

THE ORIGINAL PLAN WAS to arrange a sleepover, be the one to "find" JR dead, and have a big crying screaming terrified breakdown from it, run away into the woods before anybody could ask any real questions.

The sleepover was easy to arrange, with about six hundred paranoid phone calls from my mom, with my dad sitting there ready to tap in, his serious face on. But it had to be like that. JR's dad's this big gun nut prepper guy who's currently not working, so there was no way I was sneaking into that house. Not with locks on every door, and probably locks on the keys that went to those locks. No ceramic frogs for him. More like land mines.

Still, prepper or not, he didn't deserve Manny's big hand coming down on him, all his bullets puny and useless against a giant department-store kaiju. Neither did JR's mom, the home nurse, and neither did his little sister, Gwen. *Nobody* deserves that hand coming down on them, I mean, but nobody especially deserves it just for having JR or me for a son, for a brother. It wasn't them who walked away from Manny at the end of that summer, it was us. Cause and effect, action and inevitable reaction, man, knocking us down like dominoes.

Anyway, the way this night was *supposed* to have gone—part one was hiding the distributor caps for both my mom's minivan and my dad's truck, so that when I ran off into the woods, they'd be the last ones to show up. This was important, because I didn't want to hear my mom calling out into the trees for me, right? What kid can not stop running away when he hears that?

Next was just to come over to spend the night as usual, like a hundred other times, JR's dad swinging by to pick me up like he always volunteered to do. Like a hundred other times, too, nobody would check my backpack for any items I'd have to explain. And even if they had, right? I had, what, a cheap Halloween mask I was probably only carrying for if I started crying, couldn't stop? I had some underwear and an extra shirt like my mom always insists on, I had a coil of green string probably left over from some school project, and I had a toothbrush wrapped in Saran wrap because I can never get the baggies to seal? No knives, no guns, no lists of what to do and when, no big long notes explaining everything from the movie prank on up.

I mean, that list existed, for sure, but it was in my head. So, after settling in with whatever JR's dad cooked, which was guaranteed to be the best last meal ever, because that's the way he'd always been doing their dinners since he got fired, like he could prove himself at the table if not the car lot, after dinner my plan was to pop in the third installment of the superhero series I'd rented special on DVD, to keep everything the same as the other times, like this wouldn't work without that movie playing, like the movie was the cause of it, really. Not me, the movie. If that movie hadn't been playing, all those kids might have lived, right?

Next was to wait JR out, the guy who can famously never make it through a two-hour movie without conking, much less a three-hour epic that makes you keep the previous two playing in your head the whole time, so you can't remember who's alive again and who's still dead.

After that, just slip the mask on, watch his chest rise and fall, rise and fall. I planned on giving myself time to reconsider, yes. JR was, I thought then, the last of us except for me. Did I really and for sure want to rub all of us out of existence, just like that? Like we never even were?

It was never about *us*, though, that's what I kept having to remember, even in the moment. It was about the little brothers and little sisters who still needed to grow up, it was about the moms and dads who never did a single thing wrong, except for the usual parent stuff they couldn't help. All I'd been doing ever since Shanna, it was saving lives left and right. Yeah, the superhero movie was on DVD in my bag, but I was also *in* a superhero movie, *as* that superhero. Not the one everybody wants, no, but real life isn't always like the movies. Sometimes the real heroes, the sacrifice they make is their own legend or memory, or even their life, right? Sometimes the way you know you've done good is that the whole town hates you and wants you dead. That there even *are* still people to hate you and want you dead, that's success right there.

Anyway, JR. Instead of using the glow string—I wasn't sure, in this closed-door situation, that I'd be able to flush it, be able to keep it from matching up with the telltale welt around JR's neck—this time I was just going to unwind a wire clothes hanger from his closet. You know how sometimes where the big machine at the factory cut them off they'll still be sharp enough to grab your skin, tear your finger open while you're hanging shirts up? I'd feel along the pole for one of those ones, and probably let the shirt fall on the floor. Nobody was going to be thinking about shirts in the morning.

So, after unwinding it with just my fingers then bending it as straight as I could, I could either stab it down into JR's ear, or up his nose. Both are, as near as I could search up, direct avenues to the brain. I finally decided on the nose, since that's one of the ways they used to do lobotomies—thanks, internet—and I knew that whatever you hit when you pushed high enough and hard enough, it kind of mellows the patient out permanent. With a wire in the ear, I wasn't so sure. I might just be tearing through memories or a list of colors or something, giving JR's hands time to come up and fight this, bring his dad down on me.

The nose, then. And I was going to have to remember to *swirl* once I punched through whatever membrane was at the top of that nasal passage, the kind of swirl that would take my whole shoulder, to get as much movement at the other end of that clothes hanger as possible, which would be a kindness, like. Because this was JR. And, because the injuries would be internal, not visible, nobody would think to look for the guilty clothes hanger hidden under the carpet or wherever, and I could blast off into the woods like I was supposed to.

But of course I never got the chance.

Blame JR's dad.

I was already running my hand along the top of JR's nice shirts in his closet when his dad's voice boomed through the house for us to pile in, he was taking us to the movies, popcorn all around.

"Shanna's theater?" I asked.

"Fate," JR said, and I understood: the drive-in ten or fifteen miles out into the scrub. Ten or fifteen miles from the lake.

"O-kay . . ." I said, maybe liking this.

"*Listen,*" JR said when we went to his room to gear up, and leaned the side of his head to the wall between his bedroom and his parents', telling me to do the same, to listen.

From the other side, there were . . . clicks? For a bad moment I had to picture his dad snapping his legs together with dowels, his dad just wearing a torn-off human face over his mannequin one, but of course life's never that complicated. The simple explanation was that JR's dad was Armying up, same as always. Pistols and knives and probably grenades for all we knew. His dad had always been kind of out there, and, since finding the church of guns, he hadn't veered any closer to earth. I knew what he was proving with them this time, though: that he could take the last of the five—that's what JR and me were—that he could take us out in public and keep us completely safe, never mind the promises my mom had extracted from him. That was then. This was now.

Or maybe it had something to do with proving that his unemployment was unfair, I don't know for sure. But it's not like he'd been a bodyguard before, or a daycare worker. Taking down bad guys probably wasn't in the job description for "car salesman," I mean. I think, at the car lot, he'd maybe even sort of *been* the bad guy.

I would say I'll figure it out someday when I'm an adult, but, well.

Anyway, I got like a literal and real chill when we eased up into the drive-in line, everything painted red from taillights, and I saw the movie that was playing. It was the same one we'd taken Manny to, the same one that had been playing when Shanna's window became a truck, the same one Tim had ready to watch and the same one Steve had taken Danielle to, the same one tucked into the side pocket of my bag back at JR's place.

What are the odds of that, even? The same movie popping up for each kill?

Sometimes you just know what you're doing is the only thing to be doing. That the world is conspiring all around you to make it happen, like, not just giving you permission, but herding you the direction you need to go, giving you secret nods and obvious hand signals, and getting everything out of the way so you have the clearest path possible.

So, fast-forward through JR's dad leaving the car to explain to some of the seniors about how there were *families* here, and kids in those families who didn't need demonstrations of pot smoking, JR and me along as those impressionable kids, then fast-forward through two Rockwall dads having popcorn sent to our car, which JR's dad took as the deepest possible insult, since he could *pay* for popcorn if he wanted popcorn, and get just a little bit past JR's sister, Gwen, conking out against her mom, and that sleepyhead disease spreading through the front seat, across even to JR's dad, who'd probably been up for hours polishing bullets and cleaning slides, acting out moves and shots, doing the sound effects with his mouth, his wife pretending this would all get better when he found another job.

I had to get JR alone, right?

There were too many people in all the cars beside us, too many potential witnesses, and I had to *consider* those potential witnesses too, didn't I? With JR and me both in the same place, Manny could come stomping through, casualties under every giant footprint. Accidental deaths, innocent bystanders, collateral damage. Like JR's dad had been saying to the pot smokers and beer drinkers: *families*.

You might wonder why that's what I'm all the defender of why I care about "families" so much, being a teenager and all, who's only supposed to want to get *away* from his family, but . . . do I really need to explain it? It's not that my mom and dad almost split when I was in sixth grade, my dad skidding off on the Kawasaki, my mom cooking everything in the pantry and then throwing it all way, which I guess was the year we found Manny, too, and it's not because Shanna had to go to therapy during third period for two years because *her* dad left. It's because of math: a family is usually two or three or four or five people, and each of us was only one person. Five friends *all together,* yeah, we counted as much as a family for sure if you look at it like that. But still, that's just *one* family dying, versus five *other* families, and the numbers make the decision there. It's easy, right? It's logical. It's the way I'm supposed to think. I should get a medal for thinking like that, I should be a model thinker for some public service announcement.

Anyway, so JR and me sneak out the back side window, crawling like one inch at a time for twenty minutes, and I admit I kind of let a drop or two of pee out when I made too much noise somehow and JR's dad's whole body like spasmed, his hand coming up with a pistol from who knows where. But he was still asleep. That pistol hand lowered down into his wife's lap, stayed there. And, I mean, as far as he would have known if he'd have gotten me in his sights, JR and me were just going for the bathroom, not anything secret and bad and murdery.

There was most definitely going to be a murdery part, though. The bathrooms are on the back side of concessions, and there's about six steps of darkness back there, and a whole open field beside them. In a pasture nobody cares about, when everybody's watching the magical huge movie screen in front of them, anything can happen, right?

In my front right pocket I had my trusty glow string,

the only thing I knew I could sneak out of JR's house without any certain paranoid dads freaking out and radioing in for air support, and I guess the symmetry or continuity or whatever of me using the same weapon for all of them, it was another knock of validation for all this.

We would have made it, too, I know we would have made it to that dark empty pasture, but then, as bad luck would have it, the assistant manager from the movie theater in Rockwall was in line for a popcorn refill or whatever—more likely he was there to complain about the coke/ice ratio—and he saw us seeing him, and, first, he actually recognized us, right? On top of that, he smiled like we were the best gifts ever: here were the problem cases who had messed up his weekend with his son, who had left him shorthanded at his own theater, who had never really paid for sneaking in. At least not enough.

"Um, hey, *you two,*" he said, using a tone that made everybody around look to him, then from him to us.

"What?" JR said, stepping ahead like to fight, like, now that we were on neutral ground, now that the assistant manager didn't have boss-power, the playing field could be a lot more level.

"C'mon," I said, trying to guide him away, make as little eye contact in this scene as possible, so maybe nobody would remember it.

At which point this assistant manager of a completely

different movie theater in a completely different *town* did this harsh loud little whistle. Not at us, but somehow into the big long window of the concession stand, so that the workers there stood at attention, waiting for the next order, their hands and rags and whatever on the sticky counter.

"I'm going to need to speak with your manager," the assistant manager said, looking to all these scared-straight workers but pointing at JR and me, his long fingers somehow managing to keep us there, even though he had no power in Fate, at the drive-in.

"You can't—" JR started, using the same tone he would for somebody giving us grief at the park or wherever, somebody our age, but the assistant manager cocked his head to the side like "Seriously?"

It shut JR up.

"I trust that the two of you have ticket stubs to prove you paid to get in this time," the assistant manager said, an evil grin to his voice.

"Just go knock on my dad's window, he'll show you what we've got," JR said, stepping even closer, doing his crazy-eyes thing Danielle had taught us, via her mom, that was supposed to make you not worth messing with.

"Yes, yes, take me to him, I would love to have a discussion with—" the assistant manager tried to say.

What stopped him was JR's dad wading into the

crowd, a pistol in each hand, his lips twisted into this drill-sergeant scowl.

He'd woken up, found his charges spirited away, probably in danger.

"Shit," JR said.

When you're right, you're right.

Like they were all following the same script, the concessions line fell into twenty people going twenty different ways—*Gun! Gun!*—most of them shrieking and hyperventilating and trying to hide behind whoever they could put between themselves and JR's dad.

It's a good response, right? Especially taking into account the zero-nonsense look in JR's dad's eyes, the I've-been-waiting-for-this-day look. JR's eyes hadn't been crazy at all, I could see now. Here were some real and true crazy eyes, and a twitching cheek to match, a hungry pair of trigger fingers.

"You're the one the cops already cleared?" JR's dad said, stepping forward, pressing the barrel of his Glock right into the assistant manager's head like a pointing finger.

"I was—I was—" the assistant manager said, probably trying to vomit out whatever alibi had been good enough for the homicide detectives.

This was a higher court, though. One with more immediate sentencing.

All behind us in the sea of cars, dome lights were coming on from doors opening. People were standing up to see what the commotion was over at concessions. Phones were out, documenting this for social media. Probably more than one or two laps were wet and warm.

"Maybe the city cops were hampered by certain laws and regulations surrounding *prisoner* rights," JR's dad said, his left gun swinging around to whoever had just tossed a half-full cup of coke at his shin. He considered his wet leg, came back to the assistant manager with, "Out here in the field, though, the rules can be . . . shall we say . . . *less Queensberry*?"

This had been JR's dad's go-to since forever: no Queensberry boxing rules in the alley, son. It's all about who can hurt who first, and worst.

It was nice to talk about, kind of made you puff up a little, even.

Seeing it was all different, though.

"I don't, I wasn't, we can—" the assistant manager sputtered, and then flinched with his whole body when the sound came.

It wasn't the Glock, firing its round into his head like he thought, like he *knew* it was going to be, it was the tornado siren blaring from far off, its long moan winding up and up like someone back at the courthouse or wherever was hand-cranking air pressure into it. It sounded like Fate just had one siren, and it was in the center of town. But it was enough.

The world went soft all around me, then, I swear. Soft and slow but fast and loud too, and so all at once.

"Look, look!" the assistant manager screamed, pointing, and JR's dad, which probably wasn't good training or detention practices but whatever, he looked around with everybody else, and we tracked a boxcar from a *train* tumbling in slow motion across the sky, mostly in silhouette, but definitely a real thing that was really happening.

"No, no, not yet," I whispered, and then I was pulling JR away.

The drive-in was instant chaos. Almost immediately, engines were starting, headlights were shining everywhere, and wrecks were happening, then trying to *un*happen, and making even more wrecks. All the training and drills we always got, they were out the window.

It would be the perfect place for a kid to show up dead, I knew, which, again, was the world putting this ball up on the tee for me to hit, right?

I pulled JR into the darkness beside concessions, then behind it, and then I let the glow string unfurl down from my hand like the most evil thing ever.

"Run, run!" somebody behind us said then, and pushed past, into me, knocking me to the side.

But it was too late already.

JR had seen what was in my eyes. It wasn't a flicker of light. Kind of the exact opposite.

"*You?*" he said. "You were serious about all—all that?"

"Manny's here," I said back, holding my hands out wide to encompass all this random disaster, and then, moving slow so as to hypnotize him, I reached into my shirt, came out with the mannequin mask even though it was too late for him not to know it was me under it.

"You carry him around in your *pocket?*" JR said, not believing this enough yet.

"He's all around us," I said, lowering my face to the mask. By the time I was looking through those eyeholes, the elastic strap squeezing my head, JR was scrambling away, into the wind I knew wasn't wind, was really Manny. The same as he'd thrown a boxcar through the sky in a frustration so pure it probably made him grow even bigger, he was also, I don't know, clapping his hands like in the superhero movie, and making a windstorm.

I strode after JR like the killer I am, far too dignified to resort to running, and came around the side of concessions after h im. He was hardly ahead of me, was running the opposite way everyone else was. Because—they were all running past us because the huge bright movie screen behind them, it was coming *down*, pieces were flying off. It wasn't just one humongous board like I guess I'd always default-thought, it was like three hundred sheets of plywood painted white.

Manny was doing this, I knew.

He was standing behind it, pulling it apart, finally coming for us all, and all because me and JR were standing in the middle of the place, drawing him in.

"*Wait, wait!*" I screamed up to him, to the idea of him, and then I ran, somehow knowing where each body coming at me was going to be so I could step the other way. I caught up to JR just in front of the playground that's close enough to the screen it doesn't get in the way of the movie. As kids we'd played there. I still had a scar inside my nose from the stitches from when JR had pushed me off the monkey bars.

This time it was him falling.

I had my knees down hard into his back, the glow string already around his throat, joystick handles in my hands, and I was pulling back with every muscle I had, with every pound I had, with every wish and regret I had, and the superhero movie was flickering on the few parts of the screen still up, and, and behind them, through the black boards and whatever, I saw a flash of Band-Aid-colored skin, and then, through another part of the screen, a giant painted-on eye with a movie trying to play on it.

"Look, look!" I screamed up at Manny, pulling harder, finally feeling that crunchy give I'd felt through the string with Danielle. "I'm doing it! I'm doing it!" But the only response, it wasn't from Manny. He probably can't even talk. His lips probably don't even come apart to make words.

Who spoke, she was behind me.

What she said, it was "I *know* you're the one doing it, Sawyer Grimes."

My first fear was that it was my mom, or JR's mom—who else would use my whole name like that? But the thought of either of them having to see me hunched over JR's dead body, my hands glowing with guilt, it made my eyes hot.

I turned, ready to slink away like the guilty dog I was, only . . .

It wasn't any mom, it wasn't anybody I even could have come close to expecting.

Shanna?

"What?" I said, shaking my head no about this, that if she were still alive, then that meant, it meant—

I shook my head no, this couldn't be her.

Except there she was, right?

That meat crushed into her driven-over house, it hadn't been her, it was just her two huge *dogs,* it was her mom and her sister.

As for her, she'd—she'd been knocked into the woods somehow, I guessed, had probably had amnesia for the first week or two, had been having to steal food from open cars, from backyards. But she was Shanna too, the toughest of us all, always, the best WoodScout. And . . . that bowling shirt she was wearing, it was my dad's from when his work had had a team. It was from our costume box, out in our fort behind Holy Trinity.

That's where she'd been living. Because she didn't have a family. Because somebody was killing all her friends.

I peeled the mask back, my eyes instantly crying.

"You're—you're alive," I told her.

She answered by running directly at me, and I sat back, ready to hug and be hugged. But then at the last moment before that would have happened, her knee slashed up to connect with my face, arcing my head back, sending my whole body flying.

"No, no," I told her when I could, holding my hand with the glow string out, trying to explain to her, "I was—I thought Manny had killed you, see? I thought you were the first. But, but I've only been doing all this, because . . . because if I *don't,* then he'll—then . . . he'll kill all our families, Shanna, not on purpose, he doesn't know, it'll just be on accident? But, but I've just been, ever since you—I've been *saving* everyone, right? Their families, I mean. Tim's, Danielle's—"

"JR's," she said, about JR, dead at her feet.

I wiped my bleeding nose but that just made room for more blood to keep splashing down.

I nodded yes, JR's family too, I was saving them just the same.

"Steve's family too?" Shanna added.

"He doesn't count," I told her, snuffling what I could in. "Co-collateral damage."

"Just like Manny was going to do to our families, you mean?" Shanna said, stepping forward, her hands balled into fists at her legs, fists for *me,* and on the outside I was shaking my head no, no. But on the inside—Shanna was always the smartest of us too.

She was right.

I didn't just look like Manny. I'd *become* Manny.

And, and, if he hadn't killed her, then had he even been going to kill anybody? If you take the first domino away, do all the others keep standing?

But, but: he *had* walked out of the theater, hadn't he?

"I saw him leave the movie!" I told Shanna, standing now to insist.

"I don't know what you saw, but it wasn't him," she said, close to me now. "Do you know how I know, Sawyer? *Cousin* of mine? Do you want me to *tell* you?"

I fell back away from her, away from this, my hands in the dirt, and I was shaking my head no, no, I did *not* need to hear about any mannequins in Lost and Found down at the movies, I did *not* need to hear about any mannequins wearing green visors in the break room, I did not need to hear anything *remotely* like that, thank you.

"You're lying!" I screamed at her, my own spittle misting in front of my face because I was putting everything I had behind this, to make it true.

"Let's go see right now," she said back, and in pure self-defense, just to shut her and her lies up, I slung my hand forward whip-fast, the one still looped into the glow string, and Shanna had to see it coming, it was *glowing*, had soaked up all the light from the movie, but she couldn't stop it.

The joystick handle caught her across her eyes, more on the left side I guess, but it blinded her long enough for me to run through the swirling debris Manny was throwing up everywhere, the ground actually *shaking* from his giant footsteps pounding down all around out there in the pasture. I ran, I ran harder, I fell and got up, and, worst of all, what I stumbled onto two or three rows back, it was my dad's motorcycle, right? The wrecked Kawasaki, lying there like a horse that had known I was going to need to ride away on it.

In the middle of all this swirling chaos and death, all this screaming and crazy everywhere light, my face actually went slack, matching the mask I was wearing. Not just from seeing the motorcycle again, but because I was hearing the six hundred paranoid calls from my house to JR's all over again. The calls about the sleepover.

What had happened, what had to have happened, was they'd called JR's dad on his cell, finally found out where we were, and after all their hair-pulling and panic attacks and promises to never trust any other parents ever again, they'd taken the only ride they had, since both their distributor caps were chilling in the freezer in the garage. So—so my mom had hugged my dad's back and he'd twisted the throttle back on that death machine that was going to save my life, and they'd raced to the drive-in to save me from whoever was killing all my friends, and probably coming for me next.

I'm sorry, Mom, wherever you are. I'm so sorry, shit.

I stood the bike's bent self up, hit the starter, and only looked back when someone called my name.

It was my dad.

His hair was lifted and his shirt was torn and his glasses were gone, all from this destruction Manny was causing, all from this destruction that didn't even have to be happening.

Right now, I had to imagine, he was clomping through the playground and concessions in his huge cumbersome way, trying to catch Shanna under the cup of his two hands, the way I might try to trap a lizard. She'd tried to step in and be the final girl, the one who rises at the last moment, finds a strength she didn't know she had, but come on, right?

She was already dead.

Leaving just me.

"I have to get away, I have to go!" I screamed through the wind at my dad, my tears hot on my cheeks, under the mask, but there was too much to explain, too many lives at risk for sad goodbyes, so I just dropped my glow string at last, a gust of wind delivering it right to my dad's shin, and when he looked down at it, maybe registering it for what it was, what it had been, I stepped back, away from him, away from all of this, and screamed the bike's 750cc higher than it had ever gone then dropped the bike into first gear and peeled away, veering left and right at every last moment to avoid plowing through moviegoers trying to save themselves from the angry storm Manny was swirling up all around us. I went down the row, up another, always meaning to jump out onto the road but all I kept finding was fence and cars snarled together, people running every which way. I stood on the pegs, prairie-dogging around, finally saw the entry, its barber pole of a wooden arm lowered.

I sat back down into the seat and rocketed forward, crashed through that bar like this *was* a movie, the wood splintering on my handlebars, not sweeping me off the bike like it probably should have, if this wasn't all meant to be.

Out on the blacktop of Airport Road, with my headlight off, as in, off the *motorcycle* now, I hit eighty, I think, which was more scared than I'd ever been. It felt like if my shoes slipped off the pegs, the motorcycle would keep barreling ahead and I'd just be holding onto the handlebar, my legs flapping in the air.

When I saw the lake ten bug-pelted minutes later, I killed the engine, coasted into the movie parking lot—Shanna's theater. I parked the bike right up against the curb, a thick yellow arrow painted on the asphalt, pointing to where I was going, the world still showing me the way in case I was losing resolve at the very end, here.

I wasn't, though. Not now, not after everything I'd done to get this far.

Sixty long steps later I was on the dock, the pier, whatever, and just like I knew there had to be, somebody from the other side of the lake had rowed over to eat at Dodie's, just left their little boat tied there.

Two minutes later I was paddling that boat out here, Manny.

I know that when you're done doing what you have to at the drive-in, when the sun finally starts to rise over our town again, you're going to come lumbering across the pastures, shaking the whole world, stepping over the buildings, ducking under the high wires, and every few steps—I'm sorry for this—you're going to have to be stopping to tighten the pieces of your leg to each other.

Because of the dowels we used.

But, just come to the water, Manny. Come to the lake.

In the water those dowels can swell out, they can hold the pieces of your legs in place, right?

And, on the way, when you're pushing out through the lake, making giant swells all in front of you, probably big enough to wash cars off the bridge, then you're going to see one of your old friends out here waiting for you, just bobbing up and down, his plastic face so pleasant and lips-together just like yours always was, his hands holding tight to the side of his little boat.

It's me in here.

What I've got in my pocket now, too, it's that ticket stub Tim couldn't find for the assistant manager, that night you came back to us. This ticket isn't for that movie anymore, though. All that superhero stuff is over and done with. What I want, what I need now, what I brought this special ticket *for*—can you take me with you, please? I think I'm just about done with everybody here, except myself. I just want to, if I can, if you'll let me—I just want to go with you and sleep, and wait for the next group of kids to find us, the mannequin with the falling-apart legs and the boy mannequin beside him, his face blanked out with pleasure from all the fun that's coming.

We'll play all summer long, and it'll never go over, I know.

It can't, not as long as we're together, not as long as we have each other.

I love you, Manny. I never stopped, man.

You were the best friend we ever could have had.

Sacrifices had to be made, yeah, but that's all over now, that's all done with.

Roll credits, please.

Acknowledgments

Thanks to Larry Dobbs and my brother Spot, for the always-last-minute help with Rockwall. I've been there a lot over the years, but there's little stuff I wouldn't know if not for them. But, yeah, I still had to fudge this and that to get everything to work out. Sorry, Rockwall. Thanks to Ellen Datlow for making this one come together. She just asked a question or two like always, but they completely shaped the direction of the rewrite, made it all gel into place. And, no, I never found a mannequin in the pastures I grew up in. Everything else was out there in the mesquite, but never a mannequin. Thanks to all the X-Men I grew up with, too. There's a panel somewhere in all those issues where this giant, blank-faced Sentinel is lowering itself to the ground to try to grab a mutant. I studied and studied that panel so much, twenty, thirty years ago. I was fascinated with the Sentinel's face. Scared, too. I capitalize them like I'm doing here out of respect, I mean, because I don't want them coming for me. Which is to say, I guess, that I still feel like a mutant, all this time later. But John Darnielle's *Wolf in White*

Van was in my head as well while I was writing this. And so was Will Christopher Baer, who said once that I really had a handle on teen angst, which I'm thinking was probably a compliment? Let's just say that's what it was. Because otherwise the takeaway is that I somehow stalled out in high school. And big thanks to my son and daughter, Rane and Kinsey, slasher kids to the core—raised on them, always watching them with me, always up for talking them through, always up for one more. And, finally, thanks to my wife, Nancy, who isn't into slashers even a little but lets me follow her around the house and tell her all about this one or that one anyway, or whichever one I'm writing now, and how I'm finally going to get it right this time, really. I'm pretty sure she knows better, knows that this is never going to stop, but following her around the house talking about slashers, man: if that's not the best forever I can hope for, then I can't imagine what would be.

About the Author

Author photograph courtesy of SGJ

STEPHEN GRAHAM JONES was raised as pretty much the only Blackfeet in West Texas—except for his dad and grandma and aunts and uncles and cousins. He now lives in Boulder, Colorado, with his wife, a couple kids, and too many old trucks. Between West Texas and now, he's had seventeen novels and six story collections published. Most recent is *The Only Good Indians.* Next is the graphic novel *Memorial Ride.*

TOR·COM

Science fiction. Fantasy. The universe.

And related subjects.

*

More than just a publisher's website, *Tor.com*
is a venue for **original fiction, comics,** and
discussion of the entire field of SF and fantasy,
in all media and from all sources. Visit our site
today — and join the conversation yourself.